8/24

ADULTS
ONLY

By the same author

MORRIS GLEITZMAN

ADULTS ONLY

VIKING

The author would like to thank Mary-Anne Fahey,
James McFadyen, Isabel Angus, Jane Angus, Anna Fienberg,
Laura Harris, Christine Alesich, and the
Port Augusta School of the Air.

VIKING

Published by the Penguin Group
Penguin Books Ltd, 80 Strand, London WC2R ORL, England
Penguin Putnam Inc., 375 Hudson Street, New York, New York 10014, USA
Penguin Books Australia Ltd, Ringwood, Victoria, Australia
Penguin Books Canada Ltd, 10 Alcorn Avenue, Toronto, Ontario, Canada M4V 3B2
Penguin Books India (P) Ltd, 11 Community Centre, Panchsheel Park, New Delhi – 110 017, India
Penguin Books (NZ) Ltd, Cnr Rosedale and Airborne Roads, Albany, Auckland, New Zealand
Penguin Books (South Africa) (Pty) Ltd, 24 Sturdee Avenue, Rosebank 2196, South Africa

Penguin Books Ltd, Registered Offices: 80 Strand, London WC2R ORL, England

www.penguin.com

First published by Penguin Books Australia 2001
Published by Viking 2001
1

Copyright © Creative Input Pty Ltd, 2001

The moral right of the author has been asserted

Set in 13/15 pt Minion

Printed in England by Clays Ltd, St Ives plc

British Library Cataloguing in Publication Data
A CIP catalogue record for this book is available from the British Library

ISBN 0–670–91259–X

For Brendan and Maisie McCaul

ONE

Jake gripped his bat and stared across the ping pong table at Crusher.

Crusher stared back, not moving a muscle. Or a tattoo. The scar on the side of Crusher's face didn't even twitch.

The pine trees towering over them creaked with nervous tension.

Jake kept his expression blank so Crusher couldn't see what he was thinking.

Please.

Hit this one back.

It's not ping pong if you don't hit it back.

Crusher's eyes were black and dull.

Poor bloke, thought Jake. Must feel awful, being slaughtered by a kid.

Jake crouched over the table and did the gentlest serve he could, straight at Crusher's furry tummy.

He held his breath.

So did the seagulls hovering overhead.

So did the crabs watching from the rocks.

For a second the ball looked as though it was heading for the centre of Crusher's bat. Then a breeze wafted in off the sea and the ball started to curve away.

'Go for it,' yelled Jake desperately.

He knew that wasn't fair. You shouldn't shout things like that in ping pong. Not when you were playing with someone like Crusher.

The ball drifted past the edge of Crusher's bat and plopped onto the sand.

The crabs groaned.

So did the pine trees.

Jake's insides felt heavier than all the rocks and boulders on the island put together. He could hardly bring himself to tell Crusher the score.

'Twenty-one nil,' he said. 'That's forty-seven games to me and none to you.'

Jake tried not to show how frustrated he was feeling as he headed to the other end of the table to console Crusher.

It wasn't Crusher's fault. Crusher probably didn't even want to play ping pong.

On the way Jake overheard a crab talking to a friend.

'Poor kid,' the crab was saying. 'It's pathetic. Stranded out here on this remote island. No other kids for hundreds of kilometres in any direction. No wonder he's so lonely. No wonder he's so miserable he never even whistles any more. No wonder he's reduced to playing ping pong with a teddy bear.'

Jake turned and glared down at the crab.

'Crusher's not just any teddy bear,' he said. 'Crusher's a tough, fearless adventurer and he happens to be my best friend.'

'Oh yes, I can see that,' said the crab. 'The minute I saw you humiliate him forty-seven games to nil I knew he was your best friend.'

Jake wanted to point out to the crab that he'd tried to make things as fair as possible. He'd given Crusher a bat in each paw. And he'd done all Crusher's serves for him, even though it had been really hard work getting back to the other end of the table to return them.

But saying that stuff out loud would hurt Crusher's feelings, so instead Jake muttered, 'I just wanted to play ping pong like a normal kid.'

'Oh yes, right,' said the crab. 'It's very normal to have your ping pong opponent stuck to the other end of the table with sticky tape.'

Before Jake could reply, he was startled by a loud squawk.

He turned and saw a large seagull diving at Crusher.

'No,' yelled Jake.

The seagull clamped Crusher's head in its beak and beat its wings. There was the sound of tearing sticky tape. Suddenly Crusher wasn't stuck to the end of the ping pong table any more. His furry face was squeezed out of shape into an agonised silent scream. Jake saw the stitches pop in Crusher's face scar and fluffy stuffing spill out of the open wound.

Jake flung himself at the seagull, but it was too late. The seagull was already in the air, shooting upwards. Crusher hung from its beak, sticky tape and ping pong bats dangling at the end of his furry arms in a helpless farewell.

'Crusher,' screamed Jake.

He raced along the beach, hoping the seagull would land and he could wrestle Crusher free. But the seagull kept flying. Soon it was a dot in the sky over the ocean, heading for the horizon.

When the dot had vanished, and Jake couldn't shout any more, he collapsed onto the sand.

His only friend was gone. He was alone, a boy on a desolate rocky island in the middle of the ocean. Just him and a bunch of sarcastic crabs.

'Crusher,' he sobbed hoarsely. 'Crusher.'

'Jake,' said a voice softly. 'Jake.'

Jake opened his eyes.

He blinked a few times.

Mum was looking down at him. Behind her was his bedroom ceiling. He could feel Crusher's furry foot in his ear.

Relief flooded through him like a tidal wave of ping pong balls.

He was in bed. He'd been asleep. It had all been a dream.

'You OK, love?' Mum was saying. 'You looked like you were having a nightmare.'

'I was,' croaked Jake. 'It was horrible.'

Still blurry with sleep, he gave Crusher a hug in case Crusher had been having the same dream.

'Do you want to talk about it?' asked Mum.

Jake did, but he needed to wake up first. He squinted in the morning light pouring in through his open door. Outside he could hear the rumble of waves, the creaking of pines, the squawk of seagulls . . .

Suddenly his warm happy glow vanished. His insides started aching and it wasn't just that he urgently needed to pee.

It hadn't all been a dream after all.

The ping pong and seagull bits had been, but the island hadn't.

The island was real.

He was on it.

Mum was looking at him, concerned.

'Jake,' she said. 'Aren't you getting a bit old to be sleeping with a teddy?'

Jake realised he was still hugging Crusher. Hot-faced, he pulled away.

'He's not a teddy,' he said. 'He's a friend substitute. It's what kids have when they live on remote islands hundreds of kilometres away from other kids. Ask any psychiatrist.'

The second he'd said it, he wished he hadn't. Specially when he saw the sadness in Mum's face.

'But he's so old and grubby,' said Mum.

'It's not dirt,' said Jake. He pointed to Crusher's furry biceps. 'They're tattoos. That one's a skull with a snake coming out the eyes, and that one's a lobster with a machine gun.'

Suddenly Mum was hugging him.

'I'm sorry,' she whispered, and he knew she wasn't just talking about calling Crusher grubby. She was talking about the island and their whole lives.

Trouble was, it didn't change anything.

His life was still a nightmare and neither Mum nor Dad could do anything about it.

TWO

'Mum didn't mean to hurt your feelings,' said Jake, propping Crusher up on the kitchen bench next to the blender. 'She and Dad just get a bit thoughtless sometimes. It's the stress of running a small hotel. Worrying about whether the guests are going to fight over the last breakfast sausage or wet the beds.'

Jake switched off the blender. He could see that Crusher understood. He could also see that Crusher thought he should have put the lid on the blender first.

'Sorry,' said Jake, scraping a blob of pancake mix off Crusher's nose.

Then Jake saw something through the kitchen window that made him drop the bread knife.

A glimpse of something pink going down the cliff path.

Jake stared. The salt crusted on the window made it hard to see clearly.

It looked like a woman in a pink dress. Jake could hear Mum vacuuming upstairs, so it couldn't be her. It must be one of the guests. The woman must have climbed the wire fence with the sign on it that said 'Danger, Proceed At Own Risk'.

'She obviously doesn't have a clue how much danger she's in,' said Jake. 'I begged Dad to use the word "death" on that sign.'

Crusher looked as alarmed as Jake felt.

Jake struggled to open the window.

That's the trouble with hundred and twenty year old guesthouses, he thought as his fingers gouged at the salt-swollen metal handle. Why couldn't Mum and Dad have bought a modern motel with aluminium window frames?

Finally the old handle surrendered with a squeak and Jake pushed the window open.

He opened his mouth to yell a warning.

It was too late.

The woman was already out of sight. Jake imagined her halfway down the cliff path, clambering towards the cave. Probably clutching a picnic basket. There were probably other guests with her, loaded up with rugs and books and loaves of Dad's home-made olive bread. All totally unaware they were about to die.

They'd never hear him. Not even if he yelled as loud as he could. Not with the waves crashing and the seagulls screeching.

He had to move fast. When the tide turned and the cave suddenly filled with water, they'd be doomed. Specially when they discovered Dad's olive bread didn't float.

Jake could see what Crusher was thinking. Helicopter. Wire hangers. Hover low and hook the dopey mongrels out of the water.

'Good thought,' said Jake, 'but it'd take too long. The wire hangers are upstairs and they're all tangled. And we haven't got a helicopter.'

Jake sprinted out of the kitchen and into the office.

'Dad,' he gasped. 'Quick. It's an emergency.'

Dad was sitting at his desk, hand in his jelly-bean jar, staring mournfully at a bundle of bills.

'The guests are going down to the cave,' panted Jake. 'It's nearly eleven. They'll get caught by the tide.'

Jake waited, jiggling on the spot, while Dad slowly stood up and looked out the window, which Jake knew was pointless as you couldn't even see the cave from here. Jake jiggled some more. Dad turned and put his hands on Jake's shoulders.

'Jake,' he said in the calm voice he used when guests ran out of soap. 'Don't fuss, mate. Our guests are grown adults. They're fully qualified optometrists. They've got university degrees. They'll be OK.'

'They won't,' Jake wanted to shout. 'They'll be

underwater by eleven twenty. By eleven twenty-three they'll never prescribe a pair of glasses again. Not even to a jellyfish.'

He opened his mouth, but before he could get a word out, Dad continued.

'Our guests can look after themselves,' said Dad. 'They've come here for their holiday because they want a few days without kids pestering them. Anyway, they won't have gone down to the cave. Not after I warned them about it.'

'But,' spluttered Jake desperately, 'I saw . . .'

'First rule of hotel management,' said Dad, popping a jellybean into Jake's mouth. 'If you start seeing things, get your eyes tested.'

The phone rang.

Dad picked it up.

'Sunbeam House,' he said. 'Adults-only island resort.'

Second rule of hotel management, thought Jake as he darted towards the door, desperately hoping he could get to the cave in time. Don't let the guests drown. Specially when they're your only ones.

He crashed into Mum, who was coming into the office with the bookings book and a worried look on her face.

She frowned at Jake.

'Love,' she said, 'shouldn't you be switching the radio on for school?'

'Mum,' muttered Jake. 'It's the holidays.'

'Right,' she said distractedly. 'Sorry.'

Jake tried to slide past her, but she caught his elbow. She peered closely at him and wiped something off his forehead.

Pancake batter, thought Jake, his heart sinking. I shouldn't have turned the blender up so high.

'Jake,' sighed Mum. 'You haven't been assisting with the guests again, have you love?'

Jake shook his head. Pancake batter wasn't assisting. Not when you were just experimenting to see if your Vegemite batter tasted better than Dad's seaweed batter.

'It's an emergency,' said Jake. 'The optometrists have gone down to the cave. Look at the time.'

'We appreciate you wanting to help, we really do,' continued Mum, 'but you know you can't. Not for another few years.'

'. . . exclusively for adults,' Dad was saying into the phone. 'Sunbeam House is a sophisticated adults-only holiday hideaway. Children aren't accommodated here, so you can be sure of a nice relaxing stay.'

Suddenly Jake couldn't stand it any longer.

'They could all die,' he yelled. 'Don't you care?'

Mum dropped the bookings book.

Dad put his hand over the phone.

Jake trembled as they both stared at him, faces darkening with anger.

At least they were listening.

Jake didn't mind being sent to his room when it was for a good cause.

Like saving four lives.

He pressed his ear to the stone wall and tried to hear what was happening outside.

The waves were rumbling faintly and the seagulls were going mental as usual, but as yet there were no other sounds. No rescued optometrists stumbling back up to the house sobbing their thanks. Recommending Jake get nominated for a junior heroism award. Suggesting Dad use a bit more yeast in the olive bread.

Or if there were, Jake couldn't hear them.

'I wish these walls were thinner,' Jake said to Crusher, who'd given up trying to hear anything and was lying on the floor with his head in a pair of Jake's underpants. 'It must be fantastic living in a fibro house.'

Jake could tell from the position of Crusher's buttocks that he agreed.

And it must be even more fantastic having a room with a window, thought Jake. That was the problem with cellar bedrooms. You couldn't see out.

'With a bit of luck, Crusher,' he said, 'Mum and Dad'll be so grateful we've saved their guests, they'll give us a bedroom upstairs.'

Suddenly the door swung open.

Mum and Dad came in.

They didn't look as though they were planning

any bedroom changes. Their faces were so grim that for a moment Jake thought they'd got to the cave too late.

'Are the optometrists OK?' he asked.

'The optometrists are fine,' replied Dad in the voice he used when the meat supplier sent steak with bone chips in it. 'They're playing Monopoly by the pool. Have been for the last two hours.'

'But,' said Jake, 'I saw . . .'

'First rule of hotel management,' growled Dad. 'Check your facts first.'

Mum put a hand on Dad's arm. 'Let me do this, Frank,' she said.

Jake saw that Dad's pants were sodden from the belt down. Dad glared at Jake and sloshed out of the room.

'I saw someone,' Jake pleaded to Mum. 'I'm almost certain I did.'

Mum put her hand on Jake's cheek.

'You're a kid and kids have vivid imaginations, we understand that,' she said. 'But Jake, we need you to be a big boy. No more fairy tales, OK?'

Fairy tales?

Jake turned to Crusher to back him up. Then he remembered Crusher was a teddy bear. There were times when it was a real disadvantage having a best friend with a sewn-up mouth.

'I know it's not easy for you living here, love,' Mum was saying, 'but it's not like we keep you locked in a cupboard. You've got your own room

13

and your own TV and your own computer. You've got your schoolfriends on the radio and there are millions of kids all over the world you can meet on the Internet.'

Jake opened his mouth to explain to Mum about the people he'd met in the Internet chat rooms. How they all had names like killer and babemagnet. How their conversation consisted mostly of words like asswipe and dude.

Mum was still talking.

'All we ask, Jake, is that you be a good boy and leave the guests alone.'

'But Mum . . .'

Mum put her finger over his lips.

'Try not to argue, Jake,' she said. 'We've been through this a million times. When guests come all the way . . .'

'I know,' said Jake quietly.

There was no point arguing. He knew exactly the words Mum wanted to hear.

'When guests come all the way to a sophisticated adults-only holiday hideaway on a remote island,' recited Jake sadly, 'they don't want to find they've got to share the place with a kid.'

'Good boy,' said Mum.

After Mum had gone, Jake pulled Crusher's head out of the underpants. This was important and he wanted Crusher to hear it.

'If Mum and Dad are trying to run an adults-only island,' said Jake, 'why did they have me?'

Crusher didn't reply at first.

Jake felt panic spiralling up from somewhere under his kidneys.

Then Crusher saved him.

'They had you,' said Crusher, 'because they wanted you. Because they love you.'

Jake gave a relieved sigh.

'Right,' he said, starting to feel better already. Sometimes it was good having a best friend with a sewn-up mouth because in your mind you could make him say exactly what you wanted.

Then Jake saw what Crusher was thinking.

'You're right,' said Jake. 'If Mum and Dad want this to be an adults-only island, they should start treating me like an adult.'

Crusher didn't disagree.

'Mum's always telling me to be a big boy,' said Jake. 'Well, I'll show them what a big boy I can be. I'll show them I can be such a big boy they'll wonder how they ever ran this place without me.'

'Go for it,' said Crusher.

THREE

Jake had never organised an Easter egg hunt for other people before.

It wasn't going too well.

He crouched out of sight behind a large rock and watched the optometrists anxiously.

'I don't reckon there are any flaming eggs,' said the loudest of the optometrists, screwing up the Guest Activities Newsletter he'd found under his door that morning. He kicked a small gorse bush with his hiking boots. 'I reckon someone's having a lend of us.'

An egg-shaped object rolled out from under the bush.

'Don't be such a whinger,' said another of the optometrists. 'This is fun. I haven't been on an Easter egg hunt for years.' She spotted the egg-shaped object and pointed with her bucket. 'Look, there's one. An Easter egg.'

Jake wished it was, but he could see that it

wasn't. He sighed. Being Guest Activities Organiser was more difficult than he'd thought. He really envied Guest Activities Organisers in other hotels who could do their job without having to stay hidden.

The third optometrist hitched up his tracksuit pants and knelt down on the grass for a closer look at the egg-shaped object. It was hard and wind-dried. The optometrist picked it up and sniffed it.

'It's dog poo,' he said.

Jake realised there were some advantages to being a hidden Guest Activities Organiser. At least you didn't have to explain to guests that the poo they were holding wasn't dog poo. That some-times other guests out for walks couldn't be both-ered going back to the house when nature called.

'What I don't understand,' said the fourth optometrist, pulling a hanky from his shorts pocket and wiping his pink bald head, 'is why we're having an Easter egg hunt in September.'

Jake took a deep breath. He'd feared this might come up. He should have explained it in the newsletter.

It's because I'm usually the only one on the Easter egg hunt, he should have written. *I hide the eggs at Easter, but then I have to wait three or four months so I forget where I hid them. So I can hunt for them.*

The four optometrists were all studying the newsletter now.

'Are you sure this is an official hotel activity?' said the loud optometrist.

'I reckon it's a practical joke,' said the optometrist in the tracksuit.

The optometrist with the bucket peered at the newsletter over the top of her sunglasses. 'It says here all the eggs are hidden on this top section of the island,' she said, pointing with her bucket to the grassy patches and clumps of gorse and rocky outcrops all around. 'Come on.'

The other optometrists wandered off after her, grumbling and turning things over with their boots.

Please, begged Jake silently, watching them from behind his rock. Please find some eggs and decide this is the best fun you've had for months and then tell all your patients about it when you get back to work so they all book holidays here as soon as their new glasses are ready.

The optometrists didn't seem to be having much fun so far. The one with the bucket was looking more and more disappointed and the other three were scowling and muttering to each other.

If only I could remember exactly where I hid the eggs, thought Jake. Perhaps I could give them a clue without them seeing me.

He fumbled in his rucksack, wishing he'd brought binoculars and magnifying glasses he could leave lying around for the optometrists to use.

'Crusher,' whispered Jake, pulling him out of the rucksack. 'You were here when I hid the eggs. Can you remember where I put any of them?'

Jake waited. He knew Crusher didn't actually speak at moments like this, but the battered old bear had the incredible knack of putting the right thought into your skull at the right time.

The sun was glinting off one of Crusher's button eyes. It was like he was winking. And Jake saw that one of Crusher's arms, resting on the edge of the rucksack, was pointing down the hill.

Yes.

Suddenly it all came back.

Jake remembered where he'd hidden one of the eggs. In the bent tree halfway down the hill.

'Thanks mate,' he whispered, giving Crusher a hug. 'You're the best.'

Now, how could he point the optometrists in the right direction?

Jake peered round the rock to see where they were, and froze.

They were heading straight for him.

He squeezed down behind the rock, making himself and Crusher as small as he could.

Please, he begged. Please don't see us.

'That old wooden box next to the big rock,' said the optometrist with the bucket. 'I bet there's one in there.'

Jake felt relief flood through him like molten chocolate.

Of course.

The old weather instruments box right next to where he was hiding. It was where he'd put the biggest of all the eggs. And, he realised now, it was where Crusher had been pointing.

He heard the optometrists throw back the lid.

There was a long silence.

Jake peeped out from behind the rock.

The optometrists were staring at what was in the box.

Jake stared too.

It was definitely an Easter egg, but it had changed quite a bit since Jake had last seen it. The colour, for a start. It was green now, with black and orange things sprouting out of it. And it was furrier than Crusher. And the smell was pretty strong.

The optometrists were staggering back, hands over their mouths and noses.

'Urghhh,' said the loud optometrist, gagging loudly.

Jake realised he should probably have explained something else in the newsletter.

I made the eggs myself to save on cost, but I didn't have enough chocolate so I made some of them out of cheese.

The optometrist with the bucket was bending over. 'I think I'm going to be sick,' she mumbled through her hand.

I tried using margarine, Jake wished he'd written, *but it wouldn't hold its shape.*

'This is a fiasco,' yelled the pink-faced optometrist, who was getting redder by the second. 'I'm complaining to the management. In writing.'

Jake huddled behind his rock and wished he was in bed and that this was all just a bad dream.

But it wasn't.

He waited miserably while the optometrists stumbled down the hill. Then he put Crusher back into the rucksack and headed down the other side of the hill. He tried not to think what Mum and Dad were going to say.

Below him, the main beach stretched out, golden in the midday sun. He wished he was down there, safe and not in big trouble, like the person he could see standing in the middle of the salt haze.

Jake shaded his eyes and looked more closely.

His insides gave a jolt.

It was a girl in a pink dress.

He stared even harder.

It couldn't be a girl. The only people on the island were him and Mum and Dad and the optometrists. Even if Mr Goff had made an extra food delivery in the boat and was stretching his legs on the beach, he wasn't a girl.

This person was definitely a girl.

'Hang on tight,' Jake said to Crusher in the rucksack, and started running down towards the beach, dry grass and gorse whipping at his legs.

His thoughts were racing too. Perhaps she was a new guest. Just arrived with parents who didn't know the island was adults-only.

Then he remembered his glimpse of pink on the cliff path. The same pink as her dress. That was yesterday. So she couldn't have just arrived.

Jake was on the beach path now, feet skidding on sandy soil as he pounded his way downwards. He could see her more clearly now. Puffy short sleeves on her dress. Short dark hair. Bare feet. About his age.

She was looking straight at him.

Perhaps, thought Jake, heart hammering with effort and excitement, Mr Goff's taken on a trainee deck hand. Which would mean there'd be another kid around on the island sometimes.

At last.

Jake went through the dip at the end of the path in three big happy leaps, and when he came out from behind the dune onto the flat sand she'd gone.

Vanished.

He stared up and down the beach, dumbfounded.

She wasn't there.

Jake went over to where she'd been standing. The spot was a fair way from the waterline, even further from the dunes and a long way from the cliffs at either end of the beach. He'd been behind the dune for about three seconds. There was no way she could have covered any of those distances in that time.

Jake stood on the sand, panting and confused.

I don't get it, he thought. I just don't get it.

On the whole stretch of tide-smoothed sand there was just one line of footprints.

His.

'Un—be—liev—able,' said Dad. 'Unbelievable. Unbelievable. Unbelievable.'

Jake sat on his bed with his head in his hands.

This was worse than he'd feared.

When Dad forgot his whole vocabulary except for one word, you knew he was really upset.

'I just wanted to help,' said Jake quietly.

'Unbelievable,' said Dad, brandishing a Guest Activities Newsletter. 'Do you honestly think dragging our guests all over the island and showing them rotting cheese is helping? Do you? Do you?'

Jake shook his head.

'Frank,' said Mum. 'Let me do this. You go up, love. The optometrists'll be finishing their main course soon.'

Dad didn't move. 'Unbelievable,' he said.

Jake glanced at Crusher, who was looking even more glum than the time a guest's poodle rubbed its bottom on his head.

'Listen, Jake,' said Mum.

Jake's heart sank further. She was using the voice she used the time Mr Goff delivered a new dishwasher and dropped it.

Gentle cycle, pot-scouring strength.

'We know you wanted to help, Jake,' said Mum.

'Unbelievable,' said Dad.

'There's something we haven't told you,' Mum went on. 'Something we've been trying to protect you from. But as you're so keen to be involved, we think it's time you heard it.'

Please, thought Jake anxiously. Please don't be sick, either of you. Or getting a divorce. Or a poodle.

'Our business is in trouble, Jake,' said Mum. 'We're not getting enough guests. We haven't been for about two years. We think it's all the flash new children-not-welcome colonial cottages opening up on the mainland. Which is why, love, we can't have you upsetting the guests we do have.'

Jake digested this.

He looked down at Crusher, who was lying on the floor staring at a shoe. Crusher couldn't meet Mum's eye either.

'We've been borrowing extra money from the bank,' Mum went on. 'Last week they said no more.'

Jake looked up at her and Dad.

He waited a moment till his voice came back.

'Why don't we sell?' said Jake. 'Why don't we sell this place and leave the island and buy a motel on the mainland with aluminium window frames?'

For a few seconds there was silence in the room except for the happy pictures roaring through Jake's head.

Him and Crusher going to school on the mainland and making heaps of new friends.

Him and Crusher showing their new friends how to play ping pong and how to arm-wrestle lobsters and how to sink enemy submarines just using dynamite and clothes pegs.

Then Dad got the rest of his vocabulary back.

'We can't sell,' he said. 'Nobody wants to buy a business that's losing money.' He sat down on the bed next to Jake, but didn't look at him. 'Even if we could find a buyer, what we'd get wouldn't be anywhere near what we owe the bank.'

Jake stared at Crusher.

Between them they'd come up with an answer.

'We could pay the bank off,' said Jake. 'A bit each week. With the profits from the motel.'

'There wouldn't be a motel,' said Dad. 'We wouldn't have the money for a motel.'

Jake looked at Crusher.

Crusher didn't have any more answers either. Except ones that involved bursting into banks and taking large numbers of hostages.

'Twelve years ago,' said Mum, 'when Dad and I first came here, we had to buy a fifty year lease on this place. That's like paying fifty years rent in advance. We borrowed a huge amount of money. It was fine while this place was making good profits. But now the bank wants it all back.'

'If we can't get more guests,' said Dad, turning to look hard at Jake, 'and don't stop upsetting the ones we've got, we're history.'

After Jake finished the sandwich Mum brought him, he tried to think.

It was no good. At times like this you could only think clearly on the beach.

He grabbed Crusher and crept out of his room and up the cellar steps to the side garden.

Crusher was giving him a warning look.

'It's OK,' Jake whispered. 'I know we're meant to stay in our room. But our beach is almost part of our room, eh? Mum and Dad send us there as much as our room.'

Crusher didn't argue.

Jake looked around the side garden. Nobody was watching. He squeezed through the hedge into the ti-tree grove, ducked expertly between the trunks and branches, and slithered down through the tangled undergrowth to the side beach.

It was tiny compared to the main beach, but Jake didn't care. It was big enough for him and Crusher.

Jake checked that his beach toys were in their nylon string bags hanging from a tree above the tide line. Then he propped Crusher up on his favourite rock, and sat down next to him.

He could see that Crusher was pretty tense, so

he took a deep breath and started whistling some of Crusher's favourite tunes. TV theme songs mostly, with a couple of the ad jingles that Crusher particularly liked.

It usually helped. Crusher had let him know years ago that when he was tense he really liked being whistled to. Either that or being massaged by crabs.

Jake felt Crusher slowly relax. He took another lungful of crisp sea air and felt himself relax too. He was thinking more clearly already. He could see Crusher was too, which was pretty impressive for a bloke with a head full of fluff.

They both gazed out to sea.

'That girl,' said Jake. 'I definitely saw her. But she wasn't there. You know what that means, don't you?'

He was pretty sure Crusher did.

'It means loneliness is making me go mental,' said Jake. He glanced at Crusher to see if Crusher understood. 'Loneliness for another kid,' he added hastily, 'not another bear.'

He saw that Crusher did understand.

'So what we need,' continued Jake, 'is a way to get some kids here so I don't go more mental. And some more guests so crippling debts don't destroy our family.'

They both thought hard and when they finally had the idea it was so simple they laughed for ages with relief.

FOUR

Jake's first thought was to do it over the school radio.

As he headed back to his room he checked that Mum and Dad were out of the way.

All clear. Dad was in the kitchen stuffing fish for dinner and Mum was upstairs still trying to persuade the optometrists not to leave early.

Jake went down the steps to his room, sat at his desk, switched on the radio and checked that the microphone was working and that he had the right transmitting frequency.

Then he remembered it was the holidays.

I'm getting as bad as Mum, he thought, switching the radio off. No point calling the class in the holidays. They'd all be outside rounding up cattle or sheltering from duststorms or driving four hundred kilometres to the video shop.

No problem. E-mail would do just as well.

Jake switched on his computer, clicked Mail,

found the mailing list with all his classmates' e-mail addresses, and started writing.

Tired of hanging round with the same old herd? Fed up with grit in your Gameboy? Sick of getting to the video store and finding you've left your card at home? You need a holiday, and our place is the place for you. Restful exciting island holiday resort. Historic modern amenities. Great beach and rocks. Completely safe unless you're an idiot. Dad's a top cook and Mum lets you watch Satellite TV really late on weekends. First visit free. No need to book. Just turn up.

That should do the trick, thought Jake happily.

He added the e-map that Mum and Dad sent to all their guests, and clicked Send. Then he put the whole thing into Delete Message and clicked again.

Best that Mum and Dad not see it until the first of the kids from school and their families had arrived and were having a great time and were booking their holidays for next year and Mum and Dad could see that the island was going to be a massive success as a family holiday resort and that all their problems were over.

Jake stayed hidden behind a pile of stuff covered with a tarpaulin while Mr Goff tied the boat up at the jetty. He didn't want Dad suddenly appearing with the optometrists' bags and seeing what he was up to.

Mr Goff hauled a metal trolley out of the big luggage compartment behind the passenger cabin and came down the gangplank and over to the pile.

Perfect, thought Jake. I can talk to Mr Goff here, behind this stuff, out of sight of the house.

He stuck his head round the tarpaulin.

'Psst,' he said. 'Mr Goff.'

Mr Goff jumped and looked startled. Jake thought he looked a bit guilty as well, but Mr Goff was always glancing over his shoulder anyway, so Jake couldn't be sure.

'G'day Jake,' said Mr Goff. 'G'day Crusher.'

'Mr Goff,' said Jake, 'can I have a word?'

Mr Goff looked at him for a few moments. 'Cauliflower,' he said. 'That's a word, you can have that.'

Jake smiled politely. Mr Goff had a strange sense of humour. Mum was always saying it was because he didn't have a wife to teach him good jokes. Or explain to him that boat captains should wear blazers over their nautical jumpers and not jackets from worn-out grey suits.

Jake glanced up at the house. No sign of Dad or the optometrists.

'Mr Goff,' said Jake, 'I need to tell you something. Some families are going to be coming to stay on the island pretty soon. They won't have the usual tickets, but if you could bring them over, they'll be coming back lots of times in the future and buying tickets then. OK?'

Jake waited while Mr Goff thought about this.

'Families?' said Mr Goff. 'With children?'

Jake couldn't stop himself grinning. 'Yes,' he said happily.

Mr Goff wasn't grinning. He was frowning so hard his weather-battered face had more cracks in it than a dried-out cheese Easter egg.

'This island isn't for children,' he said. 'You should know that, you poor little dope.'

Jake sighed. Mr Goff had obviously been reading Mum's brochure for the island.

'It'll be OK,' said Jake. 'They'll be with their parents. You won't have to take responsibility for them. And they'll be really well behaved and won't get chewy on your white vinyl seats.'

Jake couldn't be sure about the last bit as he hadn't seen his classmates for nearly a year, but they still sounded pretty well-behaved on the radio.

Well, fairly.

Mr Goff was looking doubtful, but Jake knew he'd come round. Nautical people just needed time to change course, like their boats. When Dad had asked Mr Goff to start catching him sea urchins and sea slugs as well as lobsters, Mr Goff hadn't wanted to at first. He'd held out for days, right up until he'd found out how much Dad was prepared to pay him.

'Thanks, Mr Goff,' said Jake. 'I'll get out of your way now, because the optometrists'll be here soon.'

'I haven't come for the optometrists,' said Mr Goff. 'I'm doing a garbage run.'

He nodded at the stuff under the tarpaulin.

Boy, thought Jake. Mr Goff's really let it pile up this time.

'I'll give you a hand if you like,' he said.

'No,' said Mr Goff. 'Thanks anyway, both of you.'

Jake thought he looked a bit furtive again as he said that, but it could have just been indigestion.

'One more thing,' said Jake.

'What?' said Mr Goff.

'Have you taken on a deckhand?' asked Jake. 'A young trainee one?'

Mr Goff stared at Jake, puzzled. Jake could see he was getting annoyed. Then Mr Goff's expression softened.

'No,' he said. 'But if I ever do, you'll be the first to know. Now, get lost.'

As Jake walked up the path to the house, he had an idea. 'When the island's a big success as a family resort,' he said to Crusher, 'I'll suggest to Mum that she should pay for Mr Goff to do a hospitality course.'

Crusher thought it was a good idea.

Jake lay behind the sand dune and checked his watch.

Thirty minutes had passed.

Time for another squiz.

He stood up and peered over the dune.

The beach was still empty.

No girl.

Jake flopped back down behind the dune.

'OK, Crusher,' he said. 'I know you think I'm a dope.'

Crusher was pretending to ignore him. He was lying on his tummy doing one of his favourite things. Staring at ants really hard trying to make them faint.

'It was just an experiment,' said Jake.

It had been worth a try. To see if he could still see her. Even though he wasn't feeling mental with loneliness any more.

Crusher wasn't saying anything. Jake knew what he was thinking. It won't happen, Jake, he was thinking. You've been trying for three days.

'You're probably right, Crusher,' said Jake. 'But it helps pass the time while we're waiting for the kids from school to arrive.'

As soon as Jake came up the hill from the beach, he could see that something was wrong.

Mum was at the top of a ladder at the front of the house.

Her face was grimmer than he'd ever seen it.

'Jake,' she called. 'Come here please.'

It was the voice she'd used the time she'd caught a guest stealing sheets.

As Jake went over to her, he prayed it was nothing serious. Just let her still be cross about the optometrists leaving early, he pleaded silently, or the pancake batter on the kitchen ceiling.

Mum came down the ladder and opened her mouth to speak again, but before she could, the lawnmower roared into life.

Jake turned and stared.

Dad was mowing the lawn. The lawn he'd mowed only two days ago. Why was he doing it again? Even now Spring was here, the grass didn't grow that fast. And Dad hated mowing the lawn. He'd said recently he'd rather unclog a toilet in a guest's ensuite than mow the lawn.

And come to think of it, what was Mum doing up a ladder at eleven thirty in the morning? She always did office stuff in the morning, and washed sheets and unclogged guests' ensuites.

Then Jake saw something else that made him stare. Mum was holding a scrubbing brush and a bucket. And on the wall of the house, near one of the upstairs windows, was a small wet patch where she'd been scrubbing.

This is crazy, thought Jake. They're stone walls. They've got a hundred and twenty years worth of salt spray and wood smoke and dead moss and seagull poo on them. Cleaning a house this size with a scrubbing brush'll take years.

Something was going on.

Mum put the bucket down and pulled a piece of paper from the back pocket of her jeans. She unfolded it and thrust it towards Jake.

The wind coming off the ocean suddenly felt colder. Jake shivered. This wasn't about the optometrists or the batter.

Dad turned off the lawnmower and came over.

'Jake,' said Mum. 'Did you send this?'

Jake saw that printed on the piece of paper was his e-mail to the class.

His guts felt colder than the wet stone Mum had been scrubbing.

How had Mum and Dad found it? He'd deleted it. The only way they could have seen it was if . . . was if . . .

His throat was suddenly dry with excitement.

. . . *someone had replied.*

He leant forward and tried to see more closely what else was on the piece of paper. He caught a glimpse of another printed e-mail.

A reply.

Yes.

'Well,' said Dad. 'We're waiting.'

'Um,' croaked Jake. 'Yes. I did.' He pointed to the piece of paper. 'I sent it to that person in my class.'

'In your class,' said Dad.

Jake nodded.

'Well,' said Mum, 'you must have got the address wrong, because it's not someone in your class who's replied.'

Jake stared at her, trying to make sense of this.

Then he got it. Some of his class lived on properties that were so big they had other people working there. Stockmen and shearers and those people who chop the testicles off livestock. One of them must have downloaded the e-mail while the family were away overnight at the video store.

Jake glanced down at Crusher.

Crusher was thinking the same thing he was. Please, please, please let the testicle-remover have kids.

Jake looked at Mum. 'The reply,' he said. 'Is it from a testicle-remover?'

'No,' she said. 'It's from a magazine.'

Jake squinted at her. A magazine?

'A travel magazine,' she said. 'Your e-mail went to a travel magazine.'

Jake digested this. Then he realised what must have happened. The travel magazine's e-mail address must have been on the computer and he must have included it in his class mailing list by mistake.

'They're sending a journalist and a photographer to do an article about us,' said Mum.

Jake looked at Mum and Dad.

'That's good, isn't it?' he asked warily.

'Yes,' said Dad, face grim. 'It is good. It's very good. It's very very good.'

Jake waited for Mum to take over.

She didn't.

'That's why,' continued Dad, 'we're not going to punish you for trying to bring a family with children to the island. Even though it could have ruined us. Made us a joke in the adults-only hospitality industry. Had travel agents in six states wetting themselves at the mention of our name.'

'Frank,' said Mum. 'Let me do it.' She turned to Jake. 'What Dad's trying to say is we're glad you sent the e-mail.'

Jake felt confused. She didn't look that glad.

'This magazine,' continued Mum, 'is Australia's most important travel magazine. It's read all over the world. When they got your e-mail they looked us up in the travel directory. And they're really excited. They've been looking for an adults-only holiday retreat with a difference to write about for a while.'

'If it's a good article,' said Dad, 'we'll never have to worry about bookings again. Wealthy adults all over the world looking for top child-free accommodation will come flocking.'

Jake wondered why Mum and Dad weren't smiling.

He knew why he wasn't smiling.

I've blown it, he thought miserably. I've blown my one chance to make this place a family holiday resort. There'll never be any kids here now. I'm stupid. Very stupid. Very very stupid.

He could feel Crusher in his hand, limp with despair.

Then he discovered why Mum and Dad weren't smiling.

'The magazine people are on their way now,' said Mum. 'They rang this morning. They'll be here this afternoon.' She gave a stressed sigh. 'A bit more notice would have been nice, but I suppose you don't have to be considerate when you're Australia's most important travel magazine.'

Jake's head was spinning.

'They probably didn't want to give us a chance to go to any special trouble to impress them,' said Dad.

Mum and Dad looked up at the wet patch on the wall.

'Did it come off?' asked Dad.

Mum nodded.

Before Jake could ask 'did what come off?', he felt Dad's hands on his shoulders.

'Jake . . .' said Dad.

He hesitated. Jake saw him glance uneasily at Mum. She gave a little nod for Dad to continue. Jake knew what Dad was going to say next.

'Um . . .' said Dad, 'You probably know what I'm going to say next.'

'It's OK,' said Jake wearily, 'I promise I won't organise any more Easter egg hunts.'

Mum and Dad looked at each other again.

'That's a good start,' said Mum, 'but I'm afraid

we need you to promise more than that.'

'Also,' said Jake, 'I'll try really hard not to pester the magazine people.'

'I'm afraid we need even more than that,' said Dad. 'The magazine people mustn't see you. They mustn't hear you. They mustn't even smell you. They mustn't have any idea you're here. Not a peep, not a squeak, not an inkling. Understand?'

'Yes,' said Jake quietly.

'And that includes this,' said Dad.

Jake saw he was holding up a lump of pink bubblegum.

'It was under the sink in the downstairs bathroom,' said Dad. 'Another thoughtless act like that, Jake, could finish us.'

'Dad's right,' said Mum.

Jake stared at the bubblegum.

He'd never seen it before in his life.

He opened his mouth to protest bitterly that it wasn't his, that it must have belonged to one of the optometrists who was too lazy to go upstairs and stick it under his or her own sink, but before he could get the words out he saw Crusher giving him a look.

Don't bother, Crusher's look was saying. They'll never believe you. Grown-ups never believe a kid over an adult. Specially when the adult has been to university.

Jake sighed. 'Sorry,' he murmured to Mum and Dad.

'If these magazine people see a kid or a lump of bubblegum in an exclusive adults-only resort,' said Dad, 'we'll be lucky to get one star out of five.'

'It's only for a few days,' said Mum. 'We can't tell you how incredibly important this is. You do understand, love?'

'Yes,' said Jake.

Mum sighed a long and sad sigh, and Jake could see how desperately she wished the magazine people had given her more notice.

He felt the same.

He only had a few hours to send another message to all the kids at school and make sure they stayed away.

FIVE

Jake tried to head straight for his room, but Mum made him go to the kitchen and clean the pancake batter off the ceiling.

He sat Crusher on the top of the stepladder and scraped the ceiling with a cake knife.

This is ridiculous, thought Jake. If they knew how urgently I need to get on that computer, they'd be up here doing this themselves.

Perhaps he should tell them.

'Should I confess?' he asked Crusher. 'Should I tell Mum and Dad I sent e-mails inviting all the kids in my class and not just one?'

'I wouldn't,' said Crusher. 'They're under enough stress as it is.'

Jake nodded. Even though Crusher couldn't actually talk, you could always rely on him to back up your gut feelings.

'They'd only worry,' continued Crusher. 'About

what'll happen if you can't get in touch with all the kids. And half the class turns up here with their brothers and sisters. And the magazine people see them and only give this place one star out of five for not being a real adults-only retreat. And the business goes broke and we all starve and have to catch seagulls and eat them raw with our hands and paws.'

Sometimes, though, Crusher did use a bit too much detail.

Jake carried on scraping. Just as he was reaching over to get a big blob above the fridge, he saw something through the fanlight window over the kitchen door.

Dad, down the other end of the passage, coming up the steps from Jake's room, carrying something.

'My computer,' squeaked Jake. 'He's got my computer.'

Jake peered through the little window.

Where was he taking it?

Please, thought Jake. Don't let it be broken. Don't let Dad be sending it to the bloke on the mainland who repairs computers and lawn-mowers.

But Dad didn't head for the jetty. He started lugging the computer up the stairs towards the guest rooms.

Jake didn't get it.

'Back soon,' he said to Crusher, and leapt off the ladder and hurried along the passage towards the stairs. And nearly bumped into Mum.

'There you are, Jake,' she said, almost too puffed to speak.

She was carrying his TV.

What was going on?

'Jake,' said Mum, 'me and Dad want to give the magazine people the best standard of accommodation we can. We've put them in the Blue Room because it's biggest and has the best view. And we've decided they should have a TV and computer in there as well. They might want to watch "The Simpsons". Or write their article about us and e-mail it back to their office.'

Jake stared, trying to take in what she was saying.

'We'd have given them the TV from the lounge,' continued Mum, 'but then they couldn't have watched TV downstairs. And we'd have given them the computer from the office, but we need that for bookings. Sorry, Jake. Don't worry, though. Dad's put all your computer files safely onto disk.'

For a second Jake felt like going back to the kitchen and switching the blender on really high and splattering pancake batter over most of the house.

Instead he took a deep breath and reminded himself why Mum and Dad were doing this.

To save the family.

He saw that Mum was almost dropping his TV.

He hesitated for a moment, then grabbed the other end of it and shared the weight.

'Thanks, love,' said Mum.

She started climbing the stairs and Jake hung onto his end of the TV and shuffled after her.

'One other thing, Jake,' panted Mum. 'To make sure the magazine people don't see you, me and Dad want you to stay in your room for the next few days. I know it's a bit extreme, and I promise it won't ever happen again, but we think that'll be safest, OK?'

Jake didn't say anything. He took another deep breath. Then he tried to get his mind back onto more important things.

'Thanks for being understanding,' Mum went on. 'I'm sure the time'll pass quickly. You've got your books and your Gameboy and I'll make you special meals. It'll be an adventure. You can use a bucket for a toilet.'

Jake didn't reply. He was too busy trying to work out how long it would take Dad to install the TV and computer in the blue room. If Dad didn't muck around, there should still be time to e-mail the class to stay away.

Mum put the TV down on the stairs for a rest.

A short one, Jake hoped.

'I wish this could be different, Jake,' said Mum. 'I wish we could send you away. Gran's offered to have you for the week, but the fare to Darwin's more than we can come up with. We might have managed Melbourne, but Uncle Pete and Aunty Jo are on holiday in Fiji.'

Jake tried to look as though that was a shame, but mostly he was trying to remember if Dad's soldering iron was still on the blink.

'If all this works out,' Mum said, looking hard at Jake, 'we're going to make it up to you. When we get a good write-up in the magazine and start getting lots of bookings, me and Dad have agreed that if you want to, you can go to boarding school.'

Jake stared at her, stunned.

He saw how much she wanted him to be pleased.

Her forehead was crinkled earnestly under where her fringe was stuck to it with sweat, and her eyes were steady and unblinking, even though they were a bit pink round the edges as if she wasn't getting enough sleep.

Jake felt an ache in his chest. He knew it wasn't a TV-carrying ache. It was the sort of ache you get when you love someone very much and they don't really want you around.

He put his arms round Mum and gave her the longest hug he'd given her in months.

Then it just came out.

'There's something else I'd rather have,' he whispered.

'What's that?' murmured Mum.

Jake hesitated.

He'd never asked before. He'd been pretty sure it wasn't the sort of thing a kid who lived in an up-market adults-only executive retreat should ask.

'A brother or sister,' he whispered.

There was a long silence.

Jake began to wish he hadn't asked now.

Mum didn't reply, but when he felt her tears running down his cheek, he knew the answer was no.

Jake didn't get into the Blue Room for another two and a half hours.

First Dad was in there for over an hour, setting up the computer and the TV and running cables from the satellite dish on the roof and soldering his fingers.

Jake offered to help to speed things up, but when Dad had finished sucking his hand and swearing he told Jake to go and get some fresh air while he had the chance.

Then Mum vaccuumed the whole room, even though no guests had stayed in it for over two weeks. She wiped out the ensuite. She polished the computer screen and the TV screen. She put clean sheets on the bed. She put fresh flowers in the vases. She put fresh jellybeans in the bedside lolly bowls. She fetched the pictures from the walls of the other three guest rooms and hung them all on the walls of the Blue Room. She took them all down and put them back in their own rooms. She sprayed insect spray. She sprayed air freshener. Then she stood at the foot of the bed and slowly looked around the room.

Jake, peeping out of the hallway linen cupboard, teeth clenched in frustration and fingernails pressed hard into the palms of his hands, prayed she wouldn't decide to vacuum the inside of the TV or polish the chips in the computer.

She didn't.

Instead she hurried downstairs.

As soon as she'd gone, Jake darted into the Blue Room and switched on the computer.

He glanced out the window. Panic stabbed through him. Mr Goff's boat was already tied up at the jetty. Two windswept strangers were being helped out by Dad, who was doing a lot of nervous arm-waving and quite a bit of frantic bowing.

The magazine people were here.

He only had a few minutes to get the e-mail written and sent. Lucky it wouldn't need to be a long one.

Don't come.

That would do it.

Jake wanted to give the computer a shake, it seemed so slow.

Then, while he was waiting for it to boot up, he suddenly remembered something.

The chat room.

One night a couple of weeks ago he hadn't been able to sleep because he'd felt so lonely. Crusher had tried to help by suggesting they row out to sea in Mr Goff's dinghy and find a cruise ship with lots of families on board and torpedo it and invite the survivors to come and live on the island. Jake had decided it might be easier to join an Internet chat room.

He'd stored the chat room software in the utilities folder on the computer. Dad wouldn't have thought to look in there when he was moving the files. If the magazine people were investigative journalists, they might. And they'd see stuff about him.

Jake glanced out the window again. The magazine people were coming into the house. He could hear their voices downstairs.

He grabbed the mouse and went into the utilities folder and clicked furiously, getting rid of the chat room software and erasing all evidence of killer and babemagnet.

And Jake.

His head was thumping. He could hear Mum, Dad and the magazine people coming up the stairs.

It was too late. There was no time to send the e-mail. He had to get out of there. The magazine people mustn't see him.

Jake wanted to kick the computer. Why was it taking so long to shut down?

The screen went blank.

The adults were coming along the hallway. He couldn't even get back into the hallway linen cupboard. He looked wildly around the room for somewhere to hide.

Not the ensuite. Guests always needed a pee after two hours of bouncing around in the boat. Not the wardrobe. They'd be wanting to hang their pants up after two hours on Mr Goff's clammy vinyl seats.

There was only one thing to do.

Jake dived under the bed.

SIX

Four pairs of feet and ankles came into the room.

'I'll put your suitcases here,' said Dad's voice. Jake heard the suitcase racks groan as they took the weight and Dad groan as he straightened up.

'Where would you like your camera bag?' asked Mum's voice.

'Just fling it off a cliff,' said a man's voice. 'The last thing I want to think about with a wonderful view like this is a boring old magazine article.'

There was a silence. Jake imagined Mum and Dad struggling to breathe.

'Only joking,' said the man's voice. 'We'll get some great shots. Wonderful place you've got here. I can see why you decided to make it adults-only. Kids would ruin it.'

Jake huddled on the floorboards under what he hoped was the middle of the bed. As far away from the edges as possible.

'You wouldn't believe some of the places we

visit,' said a woman's voice. 'Finest hotels in the world. Sublime food. Superb service. And then you get into a lift and it's full of snotty-nosed kids with sticky mitts, giggling and farting.'

'How awful,' said Mum nervously.

Jake held his breath and begged his body to be quiet. No heart thumping. No tummy gurgling. As little farting as possible.

He peered out at the feet and ankles.

Two pairs he recognised.

He knew the ankles with bandaids on them were Mum's because she was always complaining how going up and down the stairs a million times a day made her shoes rub.

And the pants legs with the flour and quail feathers on them were definitely Dad's because he did most of the cooking.

Jake stared at the other two pairs.

Gee, he thought, magazine people don't wear very sensible shoes.

The magazine woman's brown feet and ankles were in gold sandals with very thin straps and high heels. The magazine man was wearing purple socks and lace-up shoes. The shoes didn't have high heels, but they were made from something Jake didn't recognise. Snakeskin or crocodile skin or possibly the skin of a cow with very bad pimples.

'That press release of yours was an inspired idea,' said the magazine man. 'Making it read as if a child had written it. Brilliant way to publicise a no-kids joint. Who's idea was it?'

'Um . . .' said Dad in a slightly strangled voice.

'All of ours really,' said Mum. 'I mean both of ours.'

The gold sandals took a step towards the bed.

Jake squeezed himself as small as he could.

'This house is truly charming,' said the magazine woman. 'And what a delightful room.'

'It's our favourite,' said Mum. 'Some very famous people have slept in this room.'

Please, begged Jake silently. Don't start telling them the history of the place now. He was getting a cramp in his leg. Take them for a tour round the rest of the house, he pleaded. Show them the electric can opener in the kitchen.

'We bought this place from Percival Falkiner, the artist,' continued Mum. 'The celebrities he had staying here over the years. Picasso. At least one member of the Swedish Royal Family. Roald Dahl.'

'Actually,' said Dad, 'I think that was Ronald Dahl the painter.'

'Oo look,' said the man's voice as the pimply shoes moved closer to Jake. 'Jellybeans.'

Suddenly Jake felt something tickling his nose. He knew what it was. One of the quail feathers from Dad's pants. That's the trouble with hundred and twenty year old stone houses, thought Jake as he struggled to get his hand to his face. Drafts.

He was going to sneeze.

He sneezed.

To try and stop it, he jammed his finger under his nose. The sneeze stayed silent. His head jerked up. And thumped into the bed slats.

'What was that?' said a voice above him.

Jake wasn't sure whose voice it was because his ears were ringing and panic was pounding in his head.

'Sorry,' said the magazine man. 'I must have kicked the bed when I reached for the jellybeans.'

'Don't worry,' said Dad. 'Picasso was always doing that.'

'Actually,' said Mum, 'some pretty famous people have slept in this actual bed. We had a couple here last year and I'm positive I recognised his face. From that hot chicken ad on TV.'

'Come on Maureen,' said Dad hastily. 'I'm sure our guests would like to unpack and freshen up.'

No, thought Jake desperately. They'd like a tour of the house and the garden and the beach and all the rocks.

'We hope you have a wonderful stay,' said Mum. 'If there's anything you need, anything at all . . .'

'Thank you,' said the magazine woman.

No, wailed Jake silently as he watched Mum and Dad's feet and ankles disappear out the door. Which clicked shut.

Jake heard the key turn in the lock.

It was just him. And the magazine people.

The mattress above his head creaked violently. For a moment Jake didn't know what was happening. Then he realised someone had sat down on the bed.

'I like it here,' said the magazine man as he leaned forward and undid his laces. 'No traffic, no pollution, no kids . . .'

His hand was so close Jake could see the tufts of dark hair on his fingers. If he put his head any further down . . .

Don't, begged Jake silently. Just kick your shoes off with your feet.

The magazine man kicked his shoes off with his feet. One of them spun under the bed and hit Jake in the head.

Leave it where it is, pleaded Jake, eyes watering from the pain and the smell of sweaty leather.

The magazine man left his shoe where it was.

'That boat trip was a bit much,' called the magazine woman from the ensuite. Jake wasn't sure exactly what she said next because she was peeing so loudly, but it sounded like 'If this was my place I'd send that skipper on a hospitality course'.

A desperate plan formed in Jake's mind. He could pretend he was part of Mr Goff's crew. A junior crew member doing work experience. Learning how to sail a small diesel passenger boat in rough waters and deliver seafood without being attacked by crabs.

Yes. It could work. The magazine people need never know he was Mum and Dad's son.

There was just one problem.

What was a work experience sailor doing under the bed?

Jake's excitement flopped. So did the magazine man's trousers. Onto the floor.

Put walking shorts on, begged Jake. Go for a walk round the island. Both of you.

The magazine man's shirt dropped to the floor. Followed by his underpants.

The bed creaked some more. The magazine man sighed contentedly. He didn't sound to Jake like a man going for a walk, he sounded more like a man lying down.

Jake would have sighed if he could.

'If this was my place,' said the magazine man, 'I'd build an extension along the cliff top with twenty suites, bung in a golf course and open a health spa. You couldn't lose. Fantastic views. Fantastic air. Peace and quiet and privacy. And this house is to die for.'

Jake wasn't sure, but he hoped that was good.

'We should have come here for our honeymoon,' continued the magazine man.

'Yes,' said the magazine woman, coming out of the ensuite wearing, Jake saw just before he closed his eyes, only her bra and underpants. 'Though I did quite like the Ritz-Grande Baghdad. Except the truffle soup was out of a can.'

'I'm having a little lie down,' said the magazine man. 'Fancy one?'

'Mmmmm,' said the magazine woman, 'OK.'

Jake wasn't quick enough closing his eyes again. The magazine woman's bra and underpants dropped to the floor centimetres from his face.

The bed creaked again, and kept on creaking rhythmically for what Jake reckoned was about twenty minutes.

The magazine people sighed sometimes, and moaned a bit.

Jake would have sighed and moaned too, if he'd dared make any noise. His back was killing him. And his cheeks were so hot they felt like they were cooking.

For pete's sake, he said to his cheeks. You've spent your entire lives in an adults-only retreat. You must be used to this by now. Grow up.

Finally the bed stopped creaking.

Jake waited another ten minutes or so.

Both of the magazine people in the bed above him seemed to be breathing slowly and steadily.

He hoped that meant they were asleep.

And not reading.

Or lying there with rolled-up magazines waiting for him to stick his head out.

He stuck his head out.

Nothing whacked him.

Jake slid himself out from under the bed, slowly, painfully, all his muscles stiff and all his bones aching.

He lay on the floor, listening.

A naked hairy arm was dangling over the side of the bed. Not moving.

Slowly, carefully, Jake stood up. The pins and needles in his legs almost made him fall over. He tottered a bit and remembered not to grab the bed.

He forgot not to look at the bed.

The magazine people were both sprawled on top of the sheet, asleep and naked.

Jake quickly turned away, but not before noticing that they were both a bit older and plumper than Mum and Dad.

Probably all that truffle soup.

Jake found himself in front of the dressing table, staring at the computer. It was so tempting. Boot it up, email the kids at school to change their holiday plans to Baghdad, then scram.

Tempting, but too risky.

I'll do it later, thought Jake. The magazine people will have to leave the room sometime. This evening probably, for dinner. I'll be ready.

He crept slowly to the door, careful not to slip on any underwear and do a double backwards somersault and crash to the floor.

The door was locked.

This was the tricky bit.

Jake prayed that Dad had oiled the locks of all the rooms like Mum had asked him to.

Then, slowly, slowly, Jake turned the key.

A soft click.

Jake wished the thumping in his chest was as soft.

He didn't turn to see if the click or the thumping had woken the magazine people. He'd know in about five seconds, and this way he didn't have to see the magazine woman's nipples again.

First rule of hotel management, he thought while he waited. Don't look at the guest's nipples.

The magazine people didn't wake up.

Now, he thought, slow and silent.

Jake took about three minutes to open the door. He took two minutes to step out of the room. He took another two minutes to close the door.

The hinges, oiled and in perfect condition, didn't make a sound.

Good on you, Dad, thought Jake.

He hurried down the stairs, along the passage, round the corner, and leant against the wall, legs trembling, breathing in great relieved lungfuls of air.

It had been a close thing.

The thought of going back into that room later to send the e-mail made Jake's guts curdle faster than Dad's lemon and yoghurt soup.

'What's the problem?' said Crusher when Jake

got back to his room. 'You can do it from the office computer.'

Jake remembered that the office computer didn't have the class's e-mail addresses on it.

'OK,' said Crusher. 'I was wrong. You've got a problem.'

SEVEN

'Ouch,' said Crusher.

'Sorry,' said Jake, wincing.

Crusher was tough, but there was a limit.

Jake hurriedly wiped the soap out of Crusher's eyes.

'Thanks for letting me do this,' said Jake, lathering Crusher all over.

Crusher didn't reply. Jake could see that Crusher didn't particularly like it, but that he knew Jake wouldn't be doing it unless it was important.

'It's in case Mum and Dad spring us here,' explained Jake. 'They'll want to know why I'm in the laundry instead of in my room and I can truthfully say it's because I'm giving you a bath. I won't have to say anything about being able to see the magazine people's door from here.'

The door that had been closed for nearly nineteen hours.

For the hundredth time, Jake crouched down next to the laundry sink and peered up the stairs. From that angle he could just see the bottom of the door.

It was still closed.

Jake sighed. He didn't get it.

'Why would people come all this way to a remote island,' he said to Crusher, 'and then spend nineteen hours in their room? They could have done that at home.'

'Room service,' said Crusher. 'Here they can eat paddlepops in bed without getting drips on their own sheets.'

Jake nodded. Crusher was very wise.

'Or it could be the computer,' added Jake gloomily. 'They've probably found a chat room full of writers and photographers from other travel magazines.'

Jake could see what Crusher was thinking. Run up the stairs, kick the door in, tie them up, blindfold them, send the e-mail telling the kids at school to stay away, nick off.

'Wouldn't work, Crusher,' said Jake sadly. 'If they caught a glimpse of you they'd know you were a teddy bear and that would arouse their suspicions immediately.'

Crusher looked as though he understood. He also looked a bit uncomfortable. Jake realised he'd forgotten to rinse Crusher off.

'Sorry,' he said, running clean water into the

sink. 'And sorry I had to use detergent, it's all there was.'

He plunged Crusher into the water and swirled him around a bit. Then he grabbed a towel and lifted his dripping friend out of the sink.

'Don't worry,' he said, 'I'm not putting you in the dryer. First rule of hotel management. Never put a friend in the dryer.'

Crusher didn't seem to be sharing the joke.

Then Jake saw why.

He stared in horror.

Crusher's tattoos had washed off.

Jake wished he'd never had the dumb idea of giving Crusher a bath. He'd only done it because he'd already washed all his clothes and sheets and rugs.

Poor Crusher. He looked naked without his tatts.

'Don't panic, Crusher,' said Jake. 'I know exactly where the black marker is I used last time. I'm going to find it and do you some new ones.'

The black marker wasn't where Jake thought it was.

By the time he found it down the back of his desk, he'd been turning his room upside down for over half an hour.

At least Crusher was almost dry.

Jake sat him on the lobster trap Mr Goff had

given them for Christmas, and took the cap off the marker.

'Skull and snake, same as last time?' he asked.

'Ripper,' said Crusher.

Then a thought hit Jake. He looked closely at the marker. It wasn't a permanent one. That's why the tattoos had washed off.

'Hang on,' said Jake, throwing the marker into the bin. 'We'll do them properly this time.'

He tried to remember if he'd ever seen a permanent marker anywhere in the house.

Of course.

'Dad uses a marker to label his stock cubes in the freezer,' said Jake. 'He keeps some of them for years so it'd have to be permanent.'

It was only five past eleven, so Jake knew that if he was quick he could get to the kitchen, find the marker and be back in his room by the time Mum or Dad came to the kitchen to make his lunch.

He got to the kitchen without being seen.

'So far so good,' he whispered to Crusher.

'Be careful,' whispered Crusher.

As Jake headed for the odds and ends drawer, he glanced out the window to make sure Mum or Dad weren't just outside.

And froze.

A figure was climbing over the wire fence at the top of the cliff path.

It was the magazine woman. The magazine man was already over and was helping her. He was holding a picnic basket.

Jake stared.

They must have left their room, he thought, while I was searching through mine.

Two more thoughts hit him.

One. He could duck into their room while they were gone and send the e-mail.

Two. The magazine people were heading to the cave for a picnic. The tide was about to turn. Which meant they were about to die.

'I wouldn't be holding my breath for a good write-up in that magazine,' said Crusher. 'Not if the journalist and the photographer are both cactus.'

Jake could see that Crusher was thinking the same as him. The email and the tattoos would have to wait.

Jake ran through the house, yelling for Mum and Dad.

He couldn't find them.

Crusher suggested they might be down at the jetty. Jake flung himself out the front door and peered down the path.

Crusher was right.

Mum and Dad were helping Mr Goff load what looked like old furniture onto the boat.

Jake changed his mind about involving them.

By the time he got down there and Mum and Dad got cross with him for being out of his room and he calmed them down and explained what was happening, the magazine people would be interviewing seaweed and plankton.

'We'll have to rescue them ourselves,' said Jake to Crusher. 'Without being seen.'

To have even a faint chance of doing that, Jake knew, he'd need something from under his bed.

When Jake and Crusher arrived at the cave, the magazine people were having their picnic. Jake was relieved to hear their excited voices over the surge of the turning tide.

'Look,' the magazine woman was saying. 'Quail sandwiches. And oyster tarts.'

Jake peered into the cave from behind some rocks, careful not to let the magazine people see him.

They were sitting on a small ledge at the back of the cave. The magazine woman was rummaging in the picnic basket. The magazine man was gazing out to sea, munching happily. Neither of them had noticed that water was already spilling into the front of the cave.

I've got about ten minutes, thought Jake. They should both fit in the dinghy. As long as they don't eat too many quail sandwiches.

Jake propped Crusher up in a crevice, crouched behind the rocks and heaved the big nylon bag off his shoulder. He slid out the folded-up rubber dinghy. While he unfolded it he listened to the magazine people chatting on, completely unaware he was there.

'The food here's very good,' the magazine man was saying with his mouth full.

'This morning tea is,' replied the magazine woman. 'I wasn't so sure about the breakfast. Those pancakes tasted like seaweed.'

Jake reached into the nylon bag again.

Oh no.

He stared into the bag. No foot pump.

He could see Crusher was thinking the same as him.

The foot pump must have fallen out on the cliff path. No time to go back and look for it. He peeped out from behind the rock. The water was creeping up the cave wall. In nine minutes the cave would be full of water and the magazine people would be churning around like undies in a washing machine.

Jake put the rubber nozzle of the dinghy between his lips and started to blow.

'Yummy oyster tarts,' he heard the magazine woman say.

'This is the life,' said the magazine man. 'Beautiful day, beautiful island, and my scrummy little flossy possum.'

The magazine woman gave a fond squeak. 'Bouncy bear,' she said.

For a second, Jake, blowing frantically, thought she'd seen Crusher. Then he realised she was talking about the magazine man.

Jake sucked another big lungful of air in through his nose. His chest was aching, but the dinghy was only half inflated so he ignored the pain and kept blowing.

He could see that Crusher was desperate to help, and was wishing he had lungs instead of cotton stuffing.

'Kissy kissy flossy possum,' said the magazine man.

'Big gruffy hairy bear,' said the magazine woman.

Jake found himself wishing that the cold water would reach them fairly soon.

He got his wish.

A big wave crashed in through the mouth of the cave and Jake heard the magazine woman give a yell.

'Kevin, look out.'

'Holy heck,' shouted the magazine man. 'The tide's coming in.'

Jake's lips were going numb, and his chest pain had spread to his neck, and the rocks were digging into his back, and the wind was trying to tear the almost-inflated dinghy out of his hands.

Oh well, he thought, it could be worse. Dad

could have bought me a full-size dinghy instead of just a kid's one.

The pain got worse.

'Hang on,' said Crusher. 'You're nearly there.'

Jake kept blowing.

'We're cut off,' he heard the magazine woman scream.

More water surged into the cave.

Jake blew a last lungful of air into the dinghy and pushed in the stopper. He grabbed the long nylon rope attached to one end and tied it round one of the rocks.

All he had to do now was get the magazine people into the dinghy without them seeing him.

He peeked into the cave. The magazine people were standing on the ledge, clinging to each other, water lapping around their waists.

Jake pulled out his slingshot and one of Dad's home-made Belgian chocolates. It had gone a bit soft in his pocket. Good, he thought. Won't do any permanent damage.

Still crouching behind the rocks, Jake aimed at the small bald patch at the back of the magazine man's head and let fly.

'Ow!'

The magazine man slapped his hand to his head. The magazine woman spun round to him in alarm.

While their backs were turned, Jake stood up and threw the dinghy into the cave as hard as he could. As he crouched back down, he heard it hit the water with a splash.

'Kevin,' shrieked the magazine woman. 'A boat.'

Jake stayed behind the rocks until the magazine people were safely in the dinghy. It took a while because the magazine woman tried to grab the picnic basket as it floated away and the magazine man yelled at her. Then the magazine man fell into the dinghy and the magazine woman thought he was going to puncture it with his pointy-toed shoes and yelled at him.

Finally Jake saw they were in and had worked out how to drag themselves and the dinghy out of the cave using the rope.

Jake started clambering up the cliff path so he would be out of sight when the dinghy came round the rocks.

Then he saw what was happening to the rope.

Oh no.

The knot he'd tied round the rock was slipping. It was coming undone. The rope was about to fall into the water. The magazine people would drift out to sea, possibly all the way to Antarctica. Jake didn't know much about journalism, but he was pretty sure you couldn't write a glowing article while you were being crushed by an iceberg.

He lunged at the rope, grabbed it with both hands just as it was slithering off the rock and hauled on it as hard as he could.

From the sound of the magazine people's

excited voices, the dinghy was just the other side of the rocks.

Jake felt panic stab through him.

There was nowhere to hide. The strain on the rope was too great for him to tie it up again. He had to stay there till the magazine people were safely ashore.

Which meant they'd see him.

And tell all the readers of their magazine that Mum and Dad's business was a fake and a total swindle.

Then Jake had an idea. The dinghy bag. If he put it over his head, perhaps he could pretend he was an adult. A really short adult who'd come to the island to escape the world's cruel jokes about his height.

And his kid's voice.

And his kid's legs.

Just as Jake was deciding sadly that the bag was a really dumb idea, he saw the foot pump. It was lying a little way up the cliff path.

Somehow he managed to haul on the rope even harder.

Feet scrabbling, calf muscles killing him, he struggled backwards up the slope, grabbed the foot pump while the rope nearly pulled his other arm completely off, and managed to tie the rope to the pump. Then he jammed the pump between two rocks like an anchor and flung himself up the cliff path.

Halfway up, his legs went totally numb and he collapsed behind a rock.

He squinted down at the water.

The magazine people were clambering out of the dinghy onto the rocks, laughing and crying with relief.

Jake felt like crying with relief himself.

They hadn't seen him.

Then he saw something that made the rest of him go numb.

Metres away from the magazine people, still propped up in his crevice, was Crusher.

Oh no, gasped Jake. I left him behind.

Sick with panic, he prayed the magazine people wouldn't see Crusher.

They did.

Silently, tearfully, he begged that they wouldn't go over and pick Crusher up and stare at him and wonder out loud where he'd come from.

They did.

EIGHT

Jake crouched outside the dining room window.

Indigestion stabbed through his guts.

He knew what was causing it. Guilt and sadness and worry about Crusher. That and the crumbed prawns he'd just had to gulp in his room. He'd planned to hide them in his wardrobe, but Mum had stayed to chat while he ate them.

'How was your morning?' she'd asked.

'Not that good,' he'd said.

'Never mind, love,' she'd said. 'Perhaps this afternoon will be better.'

Jake was pretty sure it wouldn't.

Not now he was peering in through the dining room window and could see the magazine people arriving for lunch.

Please, he begged the magazine people silently. Please don't assume there's a kid on the island just because you found a teddy bear. Please don't ask Mum and Dad about it.

There was a chance they wouldn't. They'd changed their clothes and they were chatting with Mum and Dad as if nothing had happened.

Jake pulled the window open a fraction so he could hear.

Perhaps it'll be OK, he said to himself. Perhaps they don't want anyone to know they ignored a warning notice and nearly drowned and had to be saved by a kid. Perhaps they just want to forget the whole thing.

In which case, thought Jake with a surge of relief, they've probably left Crusher down on the rocks where I can get him later.

Jake watched as Mum and Dad sat the magazine people down and put napkins on their laps. The magazine woman said something nice about the flowers on the table. Mum, wearing her best waitress blouse, looked pleased. Dad, wearing his best chef's hat, said something nice about the flowers on the magazine woman's frock. She looked pleased too. Although, as she pointed out, they were actually poodles.

Jake felt his indigestion wearing off.

Everything's going to be fine, he thought happily. While Mum and Dad serve the magazine people a delicious lunch of sea urchins and sea slugs, I can go and get Crusher.

He was about to turn away from the window when he saw how wrong he was.

The magazine woman reached into her bag and

pulled out something brown and furry with sad eyes and no tatts.

Crusher.

Jake's guts started hurting again.

Fighting pain and panic, he prised the window open a bit further so he could hear better.

'We found this down on the rocks,' said the magazine woman.

Jake saw the blood drain from Mum and Dad's faces.

'Oh,' said Mum, struggling to look not very interested. 'That old thing.'

'He turned up years ago while we were renovating the kitchen,' said Dad, struggling to look even less interested. 'Must have belonged to a previous occupant.'

'Really,' said the magazine woman. 'What's his name?'

Jake saw Mum and Dad glance nervously at each other.

'Um . . .' said Dad.

'Crusher,' said Mum.

The magazine people looked at each other.

'Unusual name for a teddy bear,' said the magazine man.

'Yeah,' said Dad. 'It's a long story. Um, I had this torch, see, and the bulb was loose, well not so much loose as bent, and . . .

'Let me do it, Frank,' said Mum. She smiled at the magazine people. 'We were knocking out an

74

old wall and Frank put his head into the hole and his torch went out and this teddy bear suddenly came tumbling out of an old cupboard.'

'Must have been scary,' said the magazine woman.

'It was,' said Dad. 'Specially when I got the torch working and saw a huge poisonous spider really close to my hand. Amazing thing, though. The bear had fallen on it and crushed it.'

'Which was why we called him Crusher,' said Mum.

'What a wonderful story,' said the magazine woman. 'I'm going to use that in the article.'

Jake gazed through the window at Mum and Dad with love and admiration.

Incredible. They'd just handled an unbelievably difficult situation without telling a single lie. Just the truth. Good on you, Mum and Dad.

Jake knew Crusher would be impressed too. Once the magazine woman stopped holding him upside down by his foot.

The magazine woman must have caught wind of what Jake was thinking, because she turned Crusher the right way up.

Jake tried to catch Crusher's eye.

'Sorry I forgot you,' he mouthed. Then he silently whistled a bit of the TV news theme to help with the stress Crusher must be feeling.

Crusher didn't change his expression, but Jake could tell he'd forgiven him.

'When we found him down on the rocks,' said the magazine woman slowly, fingering the scar on Crusher's face, 'we thought there might have been a child on the island.'

Jake's heart stopped.

He saw Dad's whole body sag.

Mum's jaw went tight.

'No,' she said. 'There's no child here. Absolutely not.'

'I mean,' said Dad. 'We wouldn't be calling this place adults-only if there was a kid, would we?'

Mum took Crusher from the magazine woman and reached up and put him on a shelf next to Dad's chef diploma. She kept her back to the others while she spoke. Jake could see the strain on her face.

'We had some optometrists here earlier in the week,' said Mum. 'They must have taken Crusher down to the rocks for a photo.'

'Oh,' said the magazine woman. 'I see.'

She and the magazine man turned their attention to their sea urchin salad.

Jake knew he should be feeling relieved. Mum and Dad had just saved the business. They'd just saved the family from bankruptcy and raw seagull drumsticks.

But all he could feel was sick and sad.

It's probably normal, he thought, turning away from the window. It's probably what any kid would feel after hearing his parents say he doesn't exist.

Jake lay on his bed wishing he was someone else in his class.

Anyone.

It'd be so good, not to have to hide away when visitors came. Just to go up to them and say 'G'day, I'm Jake, this is Crusher, how was the drive from the front gate, do you want to come and help us remove some testicles?'

Jake sighed and rolled over. Wishing wasn't getting Crusher rescued.

He knew Crusher would prefer a rescue plan involving helicopters and wire hangers and lots of explosions, but Jake had a feeling that pleading and grovelling would probably work better.

After a bit, he heard Mum and Dad's angry footsteps coming down the cellar steps.

'Incredible,' thundered Dad as soon as he was through the door. 'Incredible. Incredible. Incredible.'

'All we asked of you,' said Mum, white-faced, 'was to stay in your room. That's all we asked.'

'The magazine people went to the cave,' said Jake quietly. 'They'd have drowned if I hadn't rescued them.'

'Not this nonsense again,' said Dad. 'Incredible.'

Mum looked around the room as if she wanted to break something.

Finally she turned back to Jake.

'Don't make it worse,' she said. 'You've just come that close to destroying everything we've got. Don't make it worse by lying.'

Jake felt his eyes go hot with the injustice of it.

Him lie?

What about them?

They were the liars.

He forced himself not to yell at them. He knew that's what Crusher would have advised.

'Just think yourself lucky,' said Mum, 'that they only saw Crusher and not you.'

She and Dad turned to leave.

'Mum,' said Jake. 'Can I have Crusher?'

Mum looked at him, furious and weary and sad.

'Jake,' she said. 'When will you grow up?'

Jake knew he should have been working on the rescue plan, but there was something nagging at him that wouldn't let him concentrate.

What if he was wrong? What if Mum and Dad hadn't saved the business? What if the magazine people were so angry at nearly being fish bait that they were planning to write really nasty and vicious things about the island's caves and tidal movements and coastline in general?

What I need, thought Jake, is a way of drawing their attention to all the island's good features. Something that doesn't look like it's come from me.

He knew Crusher would understand that he had to do this first.

He wished Crusher was there to give him ideas.

After a lot of thinking, he came up one of his own.

Dear Maureen and Frank, he wrote.
Thanks for a wonderful stay on your island. We liked it much better than testing people's eyes. We specially liked the weather instrument box on top of the hill. It was very historic. And the sand dunes next to the main beach are great for rolling down. And that tree that the wind has bent that looks like a cat standing on its head is really funny. We particularly liked the seaweed, particularly how you can dry it and make really good wigs and false moustaches. The oysters are really good too, specially if you prod them with sticks.
Yours sincerely,
The Optometrists

That should do it, thought Jake as he put the letter on the floor outside the magazine people's room. They'll think it blew off the table further up the hallway.

It was only as he was hurrying back to back to his room that Jake remembered he'd forgotten to mention how good Mr Goff was at yodelling.

NINE

Jake opened his eyes and looked around in alarm.

It was dark.

Where am I? he thought.

He realised he was on his bed. He must have fallen asleep. The last thing he could remember was trying to come up with a rescue plan for Crusher.

Poor Crusher. Stuck on a shelf in public without any tatts. He must feel naked.

Sorry Crusher, whispered Jake. I think I'm suffering stress exhaustion. He knew Crusher couldn't hear him, not up in the dining room, but he felt better saying it anyway.

He switched his lamp on and looked at his watch.

Nine twenty.

That's weird, thought Jake. Mum hasn't brought me any dinner.

Then he remembered how angry she'd been.

The angriest he'd ever seen her. Angry enough, he contemplated sadly, to leave a kid confined to his room without food.

Jake stiffened.

Was that whispering outside his door?

It was.

Low voices, hissing and rasping and moaning.

Jake crept over to the door and pressed his ear to it. The voices stopped for a bit, then started again, quieter this time, but still with an eerie urgency to them.

Jake reminded himself he didn't believe in ghosts and pulled the door open. Even as he did a horrible thought hit him. What if it was the magazine people? What if they were still suspicious there was a kid on the island? What if they'd found his room?

Too late.

The door was open.

Jake peered into the gloom.

Standing there, looking startled, were Mum and Dad.

'What are you doing?' croaked Jake.

'We didn't want to wake you,' said Mum. 'I stuck my head in hours ago and you were fast asleep. After what you've done today, we thought you needed the rest.'

Dad was glancing anxiously up the cellar steps. 'Come on,' he said, 'let's move it.'

Before Jake could ask any more questions,

Mum and Dad grabbed an arm each and propelled him up the steps and along the passage. Jake recovered enough to start a question as they were passing the kitchen, but Mum put her finger over his lips.

'Shhh,' she said.

Jake could hear the distant chatter of the magazine people in the dining room, and the clink of cutlery. He hoped they were being nice to Crusher.

Mum and Dad sped Jake down the passage. As they passed the stairs, he glanced up. A lamp was on in the upstairs passage and Jake caught a glimpse of the patch of floorboards outside the magazine people's door.

The optometrist letter was gone.

Jake felt pleased for a moment, then a scary thought hit him.

What had Mum meant, 'after what you've done today'? Had she found the letter? Did she know he'd written it? Were they dragging him off for some terrible punishment?

The three of them were almost at the end of the passage. Up ahead was a door with a padlock on it.

Oh no, thought Jake. Surely they're not going to lock me in the storeroom? They can't be, Mum and Dad don't do things like that.

They didn't. Suddenly they steered Jake to the right and up the side passage into their bedroom.

Jake looked at them, confused. Then he saw that in the bay window at the other end of the room was a table with candles burning on it and knives and forks glinting and proper napkins.

Three places.

'Jake,' said Mum, frowning, 'we'd like you to have dinner with us.'

Jake was even more confused. Was this the punishment? Were they going to make him eat sea slugs?

'It's our way of saying sorry,' said Dad.

'And thankyou,' said Mum.

Jake looked at them, head spinning. What was going on? Had the pressure of having the magazine people here made Mum and Dad get that brain thing old people got?

'We should have believed you,' said Dad, putting his hands on Jake's shoulders. 'About the rescue. In the cave. What you did was a very brave and incredibly –'

Dad stopped.

Jake heard, in the distance, the tinkle of the dining room bell.

'You go and give them their dessert,' said Mum to Dad. 'I'll do this.'

Dad squeezed Jake's shoulders. 'Well done,' he said and hurried off.

'Come and sit down,' said Mum. She steered Jake into a chair and sat down at the other side of the table.

Jake struggled to make sense of what was happening. His thoughts felt as blurred as the candlelight.

'This afternoon,' said Mum, 'after we got cross with you, Dad went down to the cave, just to see. And he found your rubber dinghy. And a pair of purple socks drying on a rock.'

Jake stared at her. Suddenly his chest felt so light with relief it could have been a rubber dinghy as well.

Mum reached across the table and took his hand. 'You saved two people's lives,' she said. 'We're very proud of you. And very sorry. And when Dad gets back I'm going to serve you up a very special thankyou dinner.'

Jake struggled to speak. 'Did you . . . have you talked about it with the magazine people?'

Mum looked startled. 'Heavens no,' she said. 'They haven't said anything about it, so they obviously don't want us to know they ignored a warning notice and nearly drowned. We don't want to embarrass them.' She squeezed Jake's hand. 'You do understand?'

Jake nodded. He understood something else too. It must have been Crusher. Crusher must have told Mum and Dad what had happened. They wouldn't have realised he was telling them, but he must have. That's why Dad went down to the cave.

Jake glowed with love for Crusher.

Dad stuck his head into the bedroom. 'Kevin and Fiona are asking if you've dug out those photos,' he said to Mum.

'They're over there,' said Mum, pointing to the bed.

Jake saw a photo album lying on the bedspread. On top of it were a few loose snapshots.

'Kevin and Fiona asked earlier if we had any photos of the house before we renovated it,' explained Mum to Jake. 'Dad'll just whiz them down and then we'll have dinner.'

'They want you too,' said Dad to Mum. 'They want to compliment you on your mango cream tarts.'

Mum sighed. 'Sorry, Jake,' she said. 'Anything to keep them happy.'

'That's OK,' said Jake.

'Back soon,' said Dad

Jake watched Mum and Dad hurry out with the photos. It felt good, now they knew the truth. They'd have to let him have Crusher back now.

He looked at the candles. It was really nice of them to go to all this trouble. A hug and a hot dog would have done.

To pass the time he went and sat on the bed and picked up the photo album. The cover had an unusual squiggly pattern he didn't recognise.

The first few pages were mostly blank spaces except for a couple of snaps of Mum, much younger, renovating the kitchen in jeans and an old bra. She mustn't have wanted the magazine people to see those.

He turned a couple more pages. There was young Dad standing by the newly-painted front door. He was grinning and holding up a sign with wonky lettering. 'Open For Business – Adults Only'.

On the next page was a shot of young Mum sitting on a rock staring out to sea. It was a bit blurry, but something about it made Jake look again.

Not the paint in her hair. The expression on her face.

So sad.

Poor thing, thought Jake. Didn't she know you can mix turps with shampoo?

Then Jake remembered where he'd seen that look before. That terrible sad look. On the stairs when he'd asked Mum if he could have a brother or sister.

He quickly turned the page.

And found himself looking at a photo of himself. Red-faced. Bawling his head off. Naked.

Jake smiled. There were lots of photos like that in the other album, the one Mum kept in the living room.

Why was it, Jake wondered, that I was crying in every one of my baby photos?

Wind?

Indignation that they'd made me take all my clothes off?

A lens cap stuck halfway down my throat?

Jake saw that this photo had some words written underneath it. Three words, in Mum's handwriting.

He read them.

The smile dropped off his face.

He read them again, to make sure he hadn't made a terrible mistake.

He hadn't.

Suddenly he felt numb and sick.

So that's why, thought Jake. That's why I was such an unhappy baby.

Suddenly everything made sense. All the things in his life that he hadn't understood. All the things that had brought dread and fear to his days and nights.

All explained by three simple words.

TEN

Our Little Accident.

Jake stared at the words, wishing desperately Mum's handwriting was more untidy. Wishing there was a chance she'd actually written something else under his baby photo. Something that just looked like *Our Little Accident.*

But her handwriting was perfectly clear.

Our Little Accident.

That's me, thought Jake miserably. I'm their little accident.

Suddenly everything from twelve years ago was perfectly clear as well. Mum and Dad moving to the island. Setting up their exclusive adults-only guesthouse. Then disaster. A baby. Unplanned. Unwanted. A mistake. An accident.

Me.

Jake closed the photo album. His tears were making the pages wet.

It explained everything. Why would people

want a kid when their dream was to run an exclusive adults-only guesthouse? It would be like an Aussie cricket captain saying 'Yes please, I'd love a wooden leg.' Or a skydiver saying 'A concrete parachute? Mmmm, lovely.' Or a supermodel saying 'Big fat hairy buttocks, whoopee.'

Jake stopped thinking of examples. Each one was making him feel sadder.

Now he understood.

Mum and Dad hadn't wanted him.

They'd made a brave effort to hide it. All that time they'd put into washing him. Dressing him. Playing with him. Teaching him to read and not to eat insects.

They'd tried.

But they hadn't wanted him.

No wonder Mum was always so sad.

Jake dropped the photo album onto the bed. He stood up, went over to the table and blew out the candles.

'Tell me it's not true,' he whispered tearfully in the dark. 'Mum, Dad, tell me it's not true.'

Then he went downstairs to find out.

Mum saw him before he made it into the dining room.

She said something to the magazine people about a chocolate liqueur she wanted them to try, then hurried out into the passage, grabbed Jake and bundled him into the kitchen.

'What are you doing?' she hissed frantically. 'They could have seen you.'

Jake looked at her sadly. Next door he could hear Dad telling the magazine people his joke about the two rabbits and the lettuce crisper. The magazine people laughed for a long time. Things seemed to be going well.

'Mum,' said Jake. 'There's something I . . .'

Mum slapped her forehead.

'Your dinner,' she said. 'I'm sorry love, I clean forgot. Kevin and Fiona suddenly announced they wanted to interview me and Dad for the magazine. It's going really well and . . .'

'Mum,' said Jake, 'I need . . .'

'I know,' said Mum, 'I know. You must be starving, you poor love.'

She grabbed an oven cloth, handed it to him, turned to the oven, took out a plate and pressed it into his oven-cloth-covered hands.

'Fillet steak and chips,' she said. 'Your favourite. Go and start without us and we'll be there as quickly as we can. But if you get too tired, love, and you want to go to bed, we'll understand, OK?'

She kissed him on the head and hurried away.

In the kitchen doorway she stopped and looked back.

Jake saw the sad look on her face again.

'I'm sorry,' she whispered. Then she was gone.

Jake stood there, not moving. He remembered

a movie he'd seen on satellite TV. A movie about some explorers. There were three explorers at the start, then two of them shot the third. They said he was 'surplus to requirements'. Jake hadn't understood exactly what that meant.

He did now.

Slowly he turned and dropped the plate into the bin.

'Class 5F, are you receiving me?'

Nothing.

Jake fiddled with the frequency knob, turned up the transmitting volume and tried again.

'Jake Robinson to 5F. Mayday, mayday. This is an emergency. Don't come. Don't come. Don't come.'

Still nothing.

He wasn't really surprised. He hadn't really expected any of the class to be hanging around their radios at midnight in the school holidays.

'I know, I know,' Jake said to Crusher. 'An e-mail would have been better.'

Then he remembered Crusher was still a prisoner in the dining room.

He hunched over the radio again.

'Wake up 5F, this is important.'

Silence hissed in his headphones.

At least I'm trying, thought Jake miserably. That's all I can do.

He'd tried getting into the magazine people's

room, storming up there from the kitchen to send the e-mail, but their door was locked.

He'd tried going to sleep, cramming his head under the pillow, but every time he'd closed his eyes he'd seen the photo album.

This was all that was left.

'Don't come, 5F. Do not come to this island. Mr Goff was right. This island is not a good place for kids. In fact it sucks.'

More silence.

Jake didn't care. In a strange sort of way he was feeling a bit better.

'This island is a crap hole for kids. A spew bucket. Snot city.'

He knew nobody was listening, but his mouth didn't seem to mind.

'Kids would be better off going to a major war zone than coming here. A major war zone with unexploded bombs and really bad TV reception. Or a poisoned planet swirling with toxic gases and plastic bags. Or a jungle full of vicious snakes and deadly spiders and killer monkeys and desolate parched deserts.'

'I agree,' said a girl's voice.

Jake jumped so hard his headphones almost flew off.

'Pardon?' he said.

'I agree,' said the voice. It was coming over the radio.

Jake was having trouble hearing anything now,

the blood was pounding so hard in his ears.

'Jake Robinson to 5F,' he said, gripping the microphone. 'Please identify yourself.'

'Haven't got a clue what that means,' said the voice. 'I just wanted to say I know how you feel.'

'Is that you Kelsey?' said Jake, his voice sounding strange and squeaky in his headphones. 'Jody? Nicole? Leanne? Zoe?'

Even over the radio, the girl's voice didn't sound like anyone in his class.

'Got to go now,' she said. 'I'm starving.'

A friend, he realised suddenly. She could be a friend staying with one of the class for the holidays. Or a cousin. Or a trainee testicle-remover.

'Wait,' he said. 'Let's talk.'

Silence hissed in his headphones.

'Jake Robinson to person who agrees with me. Come in.'

Nothing.

Jake tried for ages, but she'd gone. Finally he turned the radio off and slumped back in his chair. He'd never felt so alone.

Or so hungry.

Power of suggestion, he thought dully. She said she was starving, so now I am. Plus, he remembered, he'd dumped his dinner in the bin.

He crept up the cellar steps and along the passage to the kitchen. He could hear laughter and merry voices coming from the dining room.

Kevin and Fiona must like the chocolate

liqueur. Mum and Dad sounded as though they quite liked it too.

Jake wondered if they'd drunk enough for him to creep in and grab Crusher without them seeing. Probably not. He'd have to wait till they were all sleeping it off and go and get Crusher then.

Jake slipped into the kitchen. He didn't plan to hang around. Grab the steak and chips from the bin, rinse them under the tap if necessary, quick burst in the microwave, and back in his room before Dad had finished saying, 'A toast to the best travel magazine in the southern hemisphere'.

But he didn't do any of that. Instead he stopped dead and gaped.

The kitchen was a mess.

Cupboard doors were open, packets and jars had been flung around, half the stuff in the fridge was on the floor. There was a trail of flour or something running out of the kitchen and along the passage.

And, he saw when he followed it, up the stairs.

Jake stood at the foot of the stairs and looked at the white trail, a dusty trickle on each step.

For a second he thought one of the magazine people must have got drunk and had an urge to make a cake and decided to do it in their room.

Then Jake realised it couldn't be that.

The magazine people were both still in the dining room. He could hear them laughing with Mum and Dad.

There must be someone else in the house.

ELEVEN

Jake followed the white powdery trail past the Blue Room and along the passage to the Pink Room. He crouched and looked closely at the floorboards.

The trail definitely ended here. Whoever made it must have gone into the Pink Room.

Probably was still in there.

Jake pressed his ear to the door.

Nothing. All he could hear was the distant sound of laughter from downstairs.

Then Jake realised what must have happened. He stood up, feeling silly. Of course. Mr Goff. He was always out fishing at night. He must have taken refuge from a storm or an angry whale. Mum and Dad must have offered him an empty guest room as long as he took his boots off before he got into bed.

Jake scuffed the floury trail with his shoe. Talcum powder probably. Mr Goff probably needed it. Cold seawater could give you a rash in some pretty uncomfortable places.

Jake turned away from the door.

Good old Mum and Dad, he thought sadly. They'll provide a bed for anyone who needs it. Even a kid they don't want.

'You coming in, Jake?'

Jake spun round.

The voice had come from inside the room.

It wasn't Mr Goff's. Mr Goff didn't have a girl's voice.

It's happening again, thought Jake. Loneliness is making me go mental again. First I start seeing things, now I'm hearing them.

'Thought you said you wanted to talk,' said the voice.

Jake took a step towards the door. He wasn't imagining this. There was someone in there.

'Please yourself,' said the voice. 'No skin off my bum.'

Jake blinked.

It sounded like the voice of the girl he'd just been talking to on the radio.

But how? The only two-way radio on the island was in his room. How could she have been talking back to him on it?

Jake tried to get a grip on himself. The voice in the room couldn't be the girl. It must be Mr Goff with a squeaky throat from too much yodelling.

There was only one way to find out.

Hands trembling, Jake pushed the door open. The worst that could happen was that he'd see Mr Goff in his undies and have to apologize.

He didn't.

The girl was sitting on the bed, cheeks bulging, chewing fast. Cradled in her arm was a plate piled with food. Between her knees was a leaking box of icing sugar.

Jake stared as she picked up a lump of chicken with grubby fingers, dipped it into the icing sugar and stuffed it into her mouth.

She was about his age, and she was wearing a faded pink dress with puffy short sleeves. Her dark hair bobbed up and down as she chewed.

Jake blinked again.

It was the girl he'd seen on the beach.

He tried to speak, but he couldn't.

She looked at him for a moment, then glanced down at her dress and brushed bits of food and clouds of icing sugar off it.

'I'm making a mess,' she said through her mouthful. 'Sorry. Haven't had chicken for years. Or cake. Or fruit. Or ham.'

Jake watched speechless as she dipped a slice of ham into the icing sugar and crammed it into her mouth.

'Or this' she said, holding up a lump of fish. 'What's this?' She plonked it into the icing sugar and squeezed it into her mouth.

'It's a sardine,' croaked Jake. 'Who are you?'

'Gwen,' she said. 'G'day.'

Jake's mind was racing. Another e-mail must have gone to the wrong address. To Gwen's parents, whoever they were. They must be camping somewhere on the island. With a two-way radio. But why hadn't they made contact with Mum and Dad? Why hadn't Mr Goff mentioned he'd brought them over?

First things first.

'Please don't get me wrong,' said Jake, 'because I'm really really pleased you're here, but there's a bit of a problem at the moment with you being in this room.'

He strained to hear if Mum and Dad and the magazine people were still distracted by the chocolate liqueur. It sounded as if they were.

The girl stood up and pushed the plate into Jake's hands.

'You're right,' she said. 'I shouldn't be here stuffing my face.'

She pulled something off the bottom of the plate and popped it into her mouth and started chewing. Jake saw a flash of pink.

Bubblegum.

Then he saw how troubled her dark eyes were.

Relax, he said to himself. Don't get panicked and scare her away. It's not such a big deal. You've got a whole island to hide her from the magazine people.

'I got carried away,' she said. 'It was being near so much food. I should be looking for my sister.'

Sister?

Jake gulped.

He knew he should have been ecstatic to hear there was another kid on the island, but at that moment all he could think about was explaining the important stuff to Gwen. Why she and her sister had to stay out of sight of all adults with funny shoes.

Before he could start, she looked him directly in the eyes.

Hers, he saw, were suddenly very sad.

'They did want you,' she said softly. 'They really did.'

At first Jake wasn't sure he'd heard right.

Then, when he decided he had, he realised she'd slipped out the door.

'Wait,' he said, and flung himself after her.

The passage was empty. Jake looked in both directions, heart thumping. Not a sign of her. She must be an incredibly fast runner.

As Jake hurried down the stairs, he prayed she wasn't a noisy one.

The adults in the dining room didn't seem to have heard anything. Not judging by their loud singing.

Jake sat on the bottom stair, breathless and dazed, Gwen's words still buzzing in his head.

They did want you.

Did she mean Mum and Dad?

How did she know?

He had to find her.

First, though, he had to clean up the mess. If Mum and Dad saw the kitchen looking like the fridge had thrown a tantrum and the stairway looking like a dandruff-sufferers convention had just passed through, they'd go ballistic.

Jake mopped and swept as fast as he could.

Lucky I'm experienced at quiet cleaning, he thought.

This was just like all those early mornings Mum let him help her while the guests were still asleep. Except at that hour Dad wasn't usually in the dining room singing the theme song from *Annie*.

A thought dribbled across Jake's mind like sardine oil across a kitchen floor. Maybe that was why Mum and Dad put up with him, because he was a good cleaner.

Jake wiped away the thought and the sardine oil, rinsed the cloth, hung it under the sink, and slipped silently out the back door into the moonlight to look for Gwen and her family.

First he went to the main beach.

If I was camping and wanted to stay hidden, he thought, I'd get in among those big dunes at the far end.

He went up the far end and shone his torch between every dune, listening carefully for the sound of voices or bubblegum popping.

Nothing.

Then he went to the high part of the island, where it started to drop away to the south. It was much windier up here for a campsite, but the view in the daytime was better if you could do without a fire.

Perhaps that's why she was so hungry, thought Jake as he checked behind the rocky outcrops. Perhaps the whole family's living off cold tinned soup.

'Gwen,' he yelled, but the wind and the crashing waves swallowed his voice.

Nothing. Not a tent, not a sleeping bag, not a billy can, not even an empty soup tin.

Jake didn't give up. But she wasn't in the forest near the jetty either, or on his beach, or in the cave.

OK, thought Jake as he plodded back up the cliff path. I give up. I must have missed them in the dark. I'll get up at first light and find them then.

Even though he was tired and cold and worried, he grinned.

Two kids on the island.

It felt good.

He knew Crusher would be excited too.

* * *

The good feeling didn't last long.

As he crept along the kitchen wall towards the back door, Jake heard voices coming from the dining room. He saw the dining room window was still a bit open, the way he'd left it earlier. Mum and Dad and the magazine people must have got sick of singing and gone back to conversation.

Jake peeped in to make sure they weren't about to head off to bed. He didn't want any tragic collisions in the hallway. Not involving him, anyway.

What he saw froze his guts.

The magazine woman was holding Crusher in one hand and a cheque book in the other.

'OK,' she was saying, slurring her words. 'Antique teddy bears are worth a bit, I know that, so I'm not going to insult you. Two hundred dollars.'

Jake stared, horrified.

She wanted to buy Crusher.

He saw Mum and Dad look at each other doubtfully.

'No,' Jake wanted to scream. 'Don't do it.'

But he couldn't risk being seen.

The magazine woman leant forward and whispered loudly to Mum and Dad. 'It's for Kevin's birthday. It's perfect for him cause he's a teddy bear too.'

'Grizzly bear,' mumbled the magazine man. 'I'm a grizzly bear.'

'Three hundred dollars,' said the magazine woman.

Mum and Dad were still looking doubtful.

They won't do it, thought Jake. Even though they'd do anything to keep the magazine people happy, they know how much Crusher means to me.

His chest ached.

He tried to catch Crusher's eye, to let him know it was going to be alright, but he could only see the back of Crusher's head.

He did some silent whistling, but he was pretty sure Crusher didn't hear it.

While the magazine people were distracted with Crusher, Dad signalled to Mum to follow him across the room to the drinks cabinet.

Jake shrank as small as he could. The drinks cabinet was right next to the window he was crouched under. He strained to hear what Mum and Dad were saying while they fiddled with the ice bucket.

'We can't,' muttered Dad. 'What about Jake?'

Good on you Dad, thought Jake.

Mum looked at Dad. Then she looked over at the magazine people, who were both kissing Crusher.

Jake shuddered. Poor Crusher. Jake wished Crusher had real stomach contents so he could throw up on them. He wished there were police on the island so the magazine people could be arrested for unlawfully kissing a family member.

'Jake's nearly a teenager, love,' Mum said

unhappily to Dad. 'He's got to say goodbye to his teddy bear sometime.'

Before Dad or Jake could react, Mum went back over to the magazine people.

'I'm afraid we can't accept your very generous offer,' she said. 'Crusher's been a part of our family for a long time, and it wouldn't be right to accept money for him.'

She took a deep breath and Jake wanted to leap through the window and hug her.

But she hadn't finished.

'So,' she said to the magazine people, 'we're going to give him to you.'

Jake lay on his bed, face pressed into his damp pillow.

Even though his tears had stopped, he still couldn't believe it.

How?

How could they have done it?

The thought was too painful, so he went back to planning the rescue operation he'd be mounting first thing in the morning.

He needed something to distract the adults while he grabbed Crusher.

Three possibilities.

One, burn the house down.

Two, blow up the island.

Three, create a giant tidal wave offshore and

wash the magazine people all the way to Antarctica.

Jake liked the third possibility best. Even though he was feeling sleepy, he thought for a long time about the best way to create a giant tidal wave.

Then he felt a hand on his shoulder.

He rolled over.

Gwen was standing there looking down at him.

Her dark eyes were shining. In the light from his bedside lamp Jake could see she was still wearing her pink dress, which he thought was strange as it was about three in the morning and she should be wearing pyjamas.

He also noticed her legs were covered with bruises. He saw why. Her shoes were thin and flat with only a wonky strap holding each one on. The soles had no grip. And the thin white socks bunched at her ankles looked hopeless for shock absorption.

That's criminal, thought Jake. Letting a kid come to an island like this with footwear like that. Poor thing must go flat on her face every time she steps on a rock.

He saw she was holding something out to him.

'This is for you,' she said. 'It cheers me up when I feel sad about not being wanted.'

Jake saw it was a doll.

He reached out and took it.

Looking at it closely, he saw its body was made

from cardboard and curtain material and its arms and legs were wooden clothes pegs and its face was drawn on with crayons.

It was smiling at him.

He felt himself smiling back. Not at the doll, at Gwen. So this was what it was like to have a real live friend.

'Thanks,' he said, looking up at her.

But she was gone.

That's impossible, he thought sleepily. She couldn't have gone that quickly.

Then he realised what must be happening.

I must be dreaming, he thought as he drifted off to sleep.

I must be dreaming.

TWELVE

'Jake, wake up.'

Jake opened his eyes and squinted in the morning light that spilled down the cellar steps.

Mum was standing over the bed, shaking him.

'I need your help,' said Mum. 'It's an emergency.'

Jake sat up, half awake.

'What?' he said. 'What's happened?'

Fragments of dreams or memories or something flickered in his mind. An explosion. A fire. A huge wave with a pair of pimply shoes floating in it. Then his head cleared and he saw the distress on Mum's face.

Suddenly he was completely awake.

'Is it Dad?' said Jake, grabbing her arm. 'Is Dad OK?'

Horrible images flooded into his head. Dad lying at the bottom of a cliff, surrounded by fragments of the rock ledge that had collapsed under him when he was picking herbs. Dad slumped in the kitchen, terribly disfigured by burning truffle oil that had ignited when he was stir-frying sea slugs. Dad writhing in agony with food-poisoning after tasting a furry green cheese Easter egg.

'Dad's fine,' said Mum, her face white with anxiety. 'It's the magazine people. They've wet the bed.'

Jake stared at her.

'Me and Dad are taking them for a walk,' continued Mum. 'I don't know how long we can keep them occupied. You've got to get the sheets changed as quickly as you can.'

Jake kept on looking at her. He didn't understand.

'The crucial thing is,' said Mum, 'they mustn't feel embarrassed. They haven't said anything about it and they obviously don't want us to. What they want is a dry, freshly made bed so they can all forget about it as quickly as possible and get on with writing nice things about us.'

Jake understood. If there was one thing more embarrassing for an adult than nearly drowning, it was weeing in the bed. The only thing worse than that, thought Jake as he swung his legs onto the floor, would be weeing in the bed and nearly drowning in it.

'Maureen.'

It was Dad, shouting urgently from up in the passage.

'Maureen, come on. Kevin and Fiona want to go on the walk now.'

Mum gave an anguished look. 'Sorry, love,' she said to Jake. 'Anything to keep them happy. Quick as you can. You know where the clean sheets are.'

Jake nodded as Mum hurried up the cellar steps.

He stayed sitting on the edge of the bed for a moment, Mum's words echoing in his head. 'Anything to keep them happy.'

Then with a stab in his guts he remembered last night. Crusher and the magazine woman and her cheque book. The terrible thing Mum and Dad had done.

I shouldn't be worrying about Dad, thought Jake bitterly. Or helping Mum. They obviously don't want me or Crusher. I should be never speaking to them again. I should be rescuing Crusher and trying to get us both adopted by a family on the mainland who aren't mean and cruel.

But he had been worried about Dad.

And he did want to help Mum.

Jake clutched at a wild hope.

Perhaps everything last night had just been a dream.

Then he felt something digging into his bottom. He reached under the sheet and pulled it out.

It was a cardboard and clothes-peg doll, smiling at him.

*　　*　　*

Jake switched off the four hairdryers and felt the mattress.

Almost dry.

Luckily the mattress protector had soaked up most of the liquid, which had covered a large area but strangely hadn't soaked in very far.

In fact, thought Jake as he hooked a clean mattress protector over the corners of the mattress, there's something weird about this whole thing.

He picked up the sheet and looked at the wet patch. It was half as big as a person. Whichever of the magazine people had done it must have a very large bladder. Even for someone who'd drunk eight litres of chocolate liqueur.

The strange thing was it didn't look like wee. First rule of hotel management, said Jake to himself. Everyone's wee is yellow. This hasn't got any colour at all.

Jake lifted the sheet to his nose and gave it a sniff.

It didn't smell like wee either. Or chocolate liqueur. Or lemon paddle-pop. It didn't smell like anything.

Jake wondered if well-off magazine journalists could afford special herbal pills that make your wee go like fresh water.

Then he had another thought.

He stuck out his tongue and tasted the sheet.

Salty.

Of course.

The magazine people must have gone for a drunken swim in the sea with their clothes on and forgotten to take them off when they went to bed.

Mystery solved.

Jake quickly smoothed a clean sheet onto the bed and did hospital corners like Mum had taught him. He flung the quilt on, straightening it out as fast as he could. Then he glanced out the window.

Mum and Dad and the magazine people were strolling back up the path from the beach. The magazine woman was showing Mum and Dad a piece of paper. Jake realised it was probably his optometrist letter.

His heart barely gave a flutter. He had more important things to concentrate on. Much more important things.

Right, thought Jake, looking around the room. Where would I put a teddy bear I'd nearly paid three hundred dollars for?

There wasn't a safe in the room. Or a bank vault.

Jake looked under the bed. Crusher wasn't there.

Send me a message, Crusher, begged Jake silently. Let me know where you are.

Then Jake had a thought.

The wardrobe.

'Thanks, Crusher,' he said.

He pulled the wardrobe door open and his heart almost stopped.

Standing in the wardrobe, staring up at him, was a little girl.

Jake took a step back.

The little girl didn't move. She didn't take her gaze off him. Her face was serious, her eyes dark and troubled. Jake, gasping for breath, remembered where he'd seen eyes like that before.

Gwen.

Under her tatty yellow dress the little girl was thinner than Gwen, but her straggly hair was just as dark as Gwen's and her eyes were exactly the same.

Was this the sister Gwen had talked about?

'Hello,' said Jake uncertainly.

The little girl's face crumpled and big silent tears rolled down her face.

'Alfonse,' she said. 'I want Alfonse.'

Jake felt panic rising inside him. He glanced out the window. Mum and Dad and the magazine people were only a short distance away from the house. If this poor little kid started bawling out loud, the magazine people would hear her in about three and a half minutes.

'Alfonse,' said the little girl.

'There, there,' said Jake, thinking desperately.

Who was Alfonse? Was that her nickname for Gwen? Or did they have a brother or uncle on the island as well?

Before Jake could think any further, his thoughts were shattered by a loud banging noise coming from downstairs.

Jake froze.

Mum, Dad and the magazine people were all outside.

So who was doing that?

He grabbed the wet bedding and the little girl's hand and hurried down to find out.

The banging was coming from his bedroom.

There was a bit of screeching as well, like old nails complaining as they were being dragged out of wood.

Jake stood at the top of the cellar steps, trying not to tremble while he stuffed the wet bedding into the laundry. The little girl's cool hand in his wasn't trembling at all. Her tears had stopped too.

Don't show her you're scared, Jake told himself. You'll only make her scared.

'Alfonse,' said the little girl sadly.

Jake felt a powerful urge to go somewhere else and look for Alfonse, but he knew he had about two minutes to put a stop to this racket.

He took a deep breath and led the little girl down the steps and pushed his door open.

The next few seconds he spent taking it all in.

His bed had been dragged to one side. Gwen was kneeling on the floor where the bed had been. She had one of Dad's big hammers. And a crowbar. She was ripping up the floorboards.

Jake took a step forward. Helping yourself to

food when you were hungry was one thing, but as far as he was concerned there was never any excuse for ripping up somebody else's floorboards.

'What are you doing?' he demanded.

Gwen looked up. She saw the little girl and sighed.

'Mabel,' she said, 'I told you to stay in the wardrobe.'

Jake saw little Mabel's eyes fill with tears again.

'That was my fault,' he said to Gwen.

He stared at the jagged hole where Gwen had already removed several floorboards.

'Sorry about your floor,' said Gwen. 'Soon as we find Alfonse, we'll be out of your hair.' She turned back to the floor, jammed the claw of the hammer under the next section of board and ripped it out.

Jake was about to wrestle the hammer away from her when he saw what was inside the hole. Stone steps, leading down into darkness. He'd often wondered why his cellar bedroom had floorboards instead of a stone floor. Dad had said it was a top layer for heat insulation, but now Jake knew the truth.

There was another cellar underneath.

Gwen put the tools down, stood up and took little Mabel's hand.

'Coming?' she said to Jake.

The two girls squeezed through the hole and disappeared from sight.

Jake stared after them. What he urgently

wanted to do was rescue Crusher. But the girls didn't have a torch or anything. And Gwen still didn't know she wasn't meant to be seen by the magazine people.

Sometimes, thought Jake, you don't do what you want to do, you do what you have to do. Crusher knew that. Jake had seen it in his eyes only recently, along with the detergent.

Jake grabbed his torch, slid his bed back over the hole in case anyone came in, crawled under and wriggled his way down into the darkness.

THIRTEEN

The steps were damp and slippery.

Jake shone his torch ahead to give the two girls some light, but they were already out of sight. The darkness didn't seem to bother them.

'Alfonse,' he heard Mabel murmur somewhere below him.

'Don't fret, sweetie,' replied Gwen. 'We'll find him.'

Jake had a thought. Perhaps Alfonse was a dog or some other pet that had escaped from their tent. A bird perhaps. Though he couldn't imagine why a budgie would want to hang out in a dark musty cellar like this.

He reached the bottom of the steps.

'Gwen,' he called softly. 'Are you OK?'

'Tops, thanks,' she said from somewhere over to his right.

Good for you, thought Jake. I've got a spider's web in my mouth and I haven't got a clue who or what we're looking for.

Perhaps Alfonse was a pet spider, but probably not.

Jake shone his torch over what looked like piles of old furniture, trying to locate Gwen so he could ask her whether they were looking for a person or an animal or an insect.

Suddenly there was a loud rattle and a scraping noise, and white light much brighter than Jake's torch made him cover his eyes.

He ducked down behind a furniture pile and squinted into the glare.

It was daylight.

A door had been opened in the far wall of the cellar.

It had been opened by an adult who now stood silhouetted in the doorway.

Hands trembling, Jake snapped his torch off. He peered around frantically for Gwen and Mabel. The cellar was huge. Shadowy heaps of furniture loomed in every direction. He couldn't see the girls anywhere.

Then he realised with a jolt that Gwen was crouching next to him, little Mabel's hand still in hers.

Jake looked at them both and put his finger to his lips in a way he hoped would encourage them to be dead silent without scaring Mabel.

He tried to see who the adult was. It looked like a man.

Dad?

The magazine man?

'Listen,' he whispered to Gwen. 'It's really important none of the adults see you two. I'll explain later. If that's not Alfonse, you'd better get out of here. I'll cover you.'

'It's not Alfonse,' whispered Gwen. She looked at Jake with a half frown, half grin. 'You're a real live one, aren't you?'

'Go,' hissed Jake. 'Scram.'

'Is anyone there?' called a man's voice.

Jake stiffened.

Then he relaxed a bit as he recognized the voice. It was Mr Goff.

Jake thought fast. Perhaps this wasn't so bad. If Mr Goff had brought Gwen and Mabel and their family to the island on his boat, he'd already know they were here. But what if he hadn't? What if Gwen and Mabel's parents had a boat of their own. Moored offshore. Which would explain why Jake hadn't been able to find their camp. If Mr Goff saw Gwen and Mabel now, he might dob them in to Mum and Dad.

Jake turned back to Gwen and Mabel to ask if their folks had a boat, but they'd already scrammed.

'Who's there?' shouted Mr Goff.

'Only me,' Jake said, standing up.

Mr Goff took a step back into the doorway. Daylight hit his face and Jake could see that his mouth was hanging open.

'Sorry if I scared you, Mr Goff,' said Jake. 'I'm looking for a pet spider.'

Mr Goff gave a doubtful growl. 'You shouldn't even be down here,' he said. 'Your parents don't want you down here. You shouldn't even know about down here.'

Why not, wondered Jake. What's so special about down here?

'I'm sorry,' said Jake, taking a step towards Mr Goff. 'I didn't know.'

His foot brushed something that rattled. Jake glanced down. It was a length of rusty metal chain. Attached to an old wooden bed frame.

Jake saw that the bed frame was leaning against a pile of other old wooden bed frames. All with lengths of chain bolted to them. Some of the chains had padlocks on the end.

Jake stared, puzzled. Why would beds need chains and padlocks on them? For a fleeting moment he wondered if Mum and Dad had experienced problems with sleepwalking guests, but that couldn't be it. There were about a hundred beds in this cellar. Mum and Dad had never had more than eight guests, not even at Christmas.

'What is all this stuff?' he asked Mr Goff.

Mr Goff didn't say anything for about a minute. He rubbed his hand over his stubbly chin and sighed a few times.

Jake got sick of watching this and had a look at more of the cellar.

There were piles of wooden desks, much smaller than Mum and Dad's in the office. And wooden benches. And some wooden frames about as tall as Jake with cracked old leather straps hanging off them. Jake didn't have a clue what they were, but they made him shiver just to look at them.

'This place,' said Mr Goff suddenly, making Jake jump, 'used to be a children's home.'

Jake turned and stared at him.

'Before your parents had it,' said Mr Goff, 'and before that artist bloke had it, this was a house of misery for kids.'

Jake moved back across the cellar towards Mr Goff, mind racing. What did he mean, house of misery?

'For about a hundred years,' continued Mr Goff, 'Sunbeam House was a place where unwanted kids were sent. Kids with no parents. Kids whose parents couldn't look after them. Kids whose parents didn't want them.'

Jake shivered again.

'Did Mum and Dad know that when they got this place?' he asked.

'Probably,' said Mr Goff. 'But not about this cellar. They only found it last year when they were clearing brambles off the side of the house. They asked me to get all this stuff over to the mainland and dump it. Without anyone seeing. Didn't want to upset the guests.'

Jake went to the doorway. He realised where he

was. The side garden he went through to get to his beach. He'd always thought this old metal door was part of the boiler room.

Why hadn't Mum and Dad told him?

Jake went back into the cellar and over to the nearest bed.

'What's this?' he asked Mr Goff, holding up the rusty chain.

Mr Goff didn't answer for another minute or so. It was hard to tell in the gloom, but Jake was pretty sure that Mr Goff's eyes were filling with tears. Mr Goff rummaged in the pocket of his jacket. Jake felt relieved. He'd been wishing he had a hanky to offer Mr Goff. But Mr Goff didn't pull out a hanky. He pulled out a boiled lolly, unwrapped it and put it in his mouth.

'The people who ran the home weren't very nice,' said Mr Goff, sucking the lolly. 'They talked about God a lot but they didn't like children very much. They specially didn't like children who needed to go to the toilet in the middle of the night.'

Jake dropped the chain, suddenly feeling not good. He hoped Mr Goff was exaggerating. Boat skippers were known for their exaggeration. Mr Goff had once told Jake he'd caught a lobster as big as a lawnmower.

People wouldn't chain kids to beds.

Would they?

Jake went over to one of the wooden frames with the leather straps.

'What's this?' he asked. He realised his voice had gone a bit wobbly.

Mr Goff didn't say anything for a bit. He looked to Jake like he'd rather be out in the middle of a raging storm battling giant lobsters.

'The people here,' said Mr Goff at last, 'used to punish the kids. Beat them.'

Jake stared at the leather straps. Awful images filled his mind. He tried to make them go away. Suddenly he felt angry at Mr Goff for making up stories like this.

'How do you know?' demanded Jake.

Mr Goff sat down on a desk and put his hand back into his jacket pocket. This time he did pull out a hanky. He wiped his eyes and blew his nose.

He turned to face Jake.

'I lived here,' he said. 'From when I was two to when I was fifteen.'

Then he put the hanky over his eyes and held it there.

Jake went over and put his hand on Mr Goff's shoulder.

'I'm sorry,' said Jake. 'I thought you were making it up.'

'I wish I was,' said Mr Goff, blowing his nose again. He unwrapped another lolly and put it in his mouth. Then he unwrapped another one and offered it to Jake.

'Thanks,' said Jake, taking it.

There was something Jake didn't understand. He wasn't sure if he should say it. He decided to anyway.

'Mr Goff,' he said. 'Why do you hang around here? If that had happened to me, I wouldn't want to keep coming back here. I'd sail off somewhere else and start a new life and have a family and never think about this place again. That's what I'd do. That's what I'm going to do.'

Jake felt himself shaking all over.

'It doesn't work like that,' said Mr Goff. 'I don't know why I keep coming back. 'Cause I'm an idiot probably. And it's my job. But one thing I do know. When you've seen kids suffer like I have, you don't want to have a family yourself. No way would I bring kids into a world that can treat them like this.'

He snatched up a bed chain and tried to tear it off the bed. It was too strong for him. Angrily he flung it back down.

Jake put Mr Goff's lolly in his mouth and sucked hard and thought even harder.

Was this why Mum and Dad didn't want me? Because they had really unhappy childhoods too? Because they didn't want me to suffer in a cruel world?

Jake tried to remember either of them ever saying anything about an unhappy childhood. All he could think of was Mum's story about how once on a family picnic when she was six she'd sat on a bull ants' nest. And Dad mentioning a couple of times that his mum used to like making oyster milkshakes.

It didn't seem much.

If there was more, why hadn't they said anything?

Jake wished Crusher was there. Crusher would think of an explanation. Crusher was really good at thinking up things, even things that didn't involve dynamite and wire hangers.

Mr Goff was lost in thought. Then suddenly he grabbed Jake's arm. 'This is just between us,' he said. 'OK?'

Jake nodded. 'Don't worry,' he said. 'I won't tell Mum and Dad.'

Mr Goff looked relieved. 'Thanks,' he said. 'Now get lost, I've got work to do.'

Jake hurried through the side garden and along the back of the house.

His head was so full of thoughts he felt dizzy. So dizzy that when he caught a glimpse of something pink on the cliff path he thought he was seeing things again.

He looked more closely and with a jolt of alarm realised he wasn't.

It was Gwen.

She was hurrying down towards the cave.

FOURTEEN

Jake's first impulse was to yell a warning.

Then he remembered that Mum and Dad and the magazine people were in the house. If they heard a kid yelling on the cliff top they'd choke on their morning tea. The magazine people would write their whole article about yelling kids.

Jake glanced at his watch. It was nearly eleven thirty. The tide had turned half an hour ago. At least Gwen wasn't in danger of drowning. All he had to do was get down there and warn her to stay out of sight.

He ran over to the wire fence, hoping nobody was watching from the kitchen. Nobody yelled, so he guessed they weren't. Unless they were having trouble yelling because of the coffee and cheese-cake coming out their noses.

Jake climbed over the 'Danger, Proceed At Own Risk' sign and headed down the path.

He couldn't see Gwen.

Oh no, he thought. At the speed she was going, if she's slipped in those useless shoes . . .

Below him the waves thundered into the base of the cliff.

Then he saw her. She was standing in the mouth of the cave, on the lip of the rock, staring into the surging water.

Jake felt relief tingle through him. He felt it for the next three or four seconds, right up till she fell forward into the water.

'Gwen,' he yelled in horror.

He scrambled over rocks to the mouth of the cave and crouched at the water's edge, trying to see her. The water was dark and Jake knew that meant deep.

Nothing, not even a glimpse of pink dress or a flash of white socks.

She'd been under for about thirty seconds. That meant she had about a minute until she drowned. If she had really tough lungs.

As Jake peered into the churning depths, he remembered the time he'd tried to break the world breath-holding record in the bath. After a minute and ten seconds he'd gasped in air so desperately he'd almost swallowed the soap.

Forty-five seconds gone.

She's got thirty seconds left, thought Jake. Thirty seconds to make it back to the surface so I don't have to dive in after her.

Ten.

Twenty.

Twenty-nine.

Jake saw something white flash to the surface. It was an air bubble.

He kicked off his shoes and dived in.

The water was colder than anything he'd ever experienced, including eating pizza straight out of the freezer.

Worse, as he plummeted into the murky depths, he felt great tidal surges grab hold of him and spin him against rocks, battering the air out of him. All he could see were bubbles. And stars.

No Gwen.

Jake tried to kick his way back to the surface, but he didn't know which way the surface was.

He started to panic.

Think straight, he screamed at himself. Don't breathe in.

Suddenly a dark shape loomed. It looked as big as a lawnmower. Jake kicked wildly, but something had him by the back of the t-shirt and was dragging him through the water.

He tried to struggle, but his legs needed oxygen to keep kicking.

Then he saw a flash of colour.

It looked like pink.

He prayed it was pink.

It was pink.

If he'd dared open his mouth he would have sobbed with relief.

Gwen.

Gwen was taking him to the surface.

Except, when he burst out of the water into blissful air, he couldn't see a thing. Not even the wet rock he was lying on. He was in total darkness.

This is impossible, he said to himself between gasping lungfuls. It can't have got dark. I haven't had lunch yet.

'Are you alright?'

It was Gwen's voice, nearby.

Echoing.

Of course. A cave.

Now Jake's brain had oxygen, it was working again.

We must be in a pitch dark cave, he realised. A cave you can only reach by going underwater. A cave that's behind the first cave.

He wished he hadn't left his torch in the cellar.

'Take my hand.'

Gwen's voice again. Jake felt her cool wet hand slip into his.

And suddenly the cave lit up. Not brightly, more of a dull eerie glow, but enough for Jake to see that it was quite a big cave with high rock walls and a dry flat sandy area at one end.

That's amazing, thought Jake, trying to see where the light was coming from. Must be glow worms. Hoping we've come to feed them.

Gwen led him stumbling onto the dry sand. His legs were still wobbly and he dropped to his knees, pulling his hand away from hers to break his fall.

The instant he did, the cave went dark again.

Glow worms obviously don't like swearing, thought Jake. Then he remembered his swearing had been silent. And so far he hadn't seen a single worm of any description.

'Here,' said Gwen. 'It's OK.'

She held his hand and as soon as she did, before his amazed eyes, the cave lit up again.

Jake looked at her and realised his mouth must be open because she was looking pretty amused at the sight.

He let go of her hand.

Dark.

He grabbed her hand.

Light.

This is incredible, thought Jake. Must be some sort of weird static electrical phenomenon. Our wet clothes must be conducting it somehow. He made a mental note, once they were out of here, to see if the phenomenon could be used to solve the world's power problems and make his and Gwen's families very rich.

Then he saw that Gwen had stopped grinning. She was frowning at him, as if she couldn't quite believe what she was seeing. Her dark eyes suddenly looked deeper than any of the water he and she had recently been in.

'Thanks,' she said softly. 'You risked your life to try and rescue me. That was very brave.'

Even though he was shivering, Jake felt suddenly warm inside.

'But,' continued Gwen, 'also a bit dopey.'

Jake didn't understand.

'You fell in,' he said. 'I had to try and . . .'

'I didn't fall,' she said. 'That was my version of a dive. I was just coming to see if Mabel was down here.'

Jake stared at her. Little Mabel, down here?

'She's been coming here when she feels like a sulk,' said Gwen. 'But she's not here now, nor's Alfonse, so we may as well go.'

She stood up and Jake, anxious not to plunge them into darkness, did too.

Gwen reached over and pulled a lump of something green off a rock.

'I was wondering where I left that,' she said.

Jake saw it was a lump of bubble gum.

She popped it in her mouth and squeezed his hand. 'Do you want to go the quick way back,' she said, 'or the fun way?'

Jake was about to say 'the safe way', then he saw the expression on her face. He'd never seen anything like it. Not once on any of his trips to the mainland for shopping or the doctor, with all the peering he'd done over school fences, had he ever seen so much glee, mystery and naughtiness on one kid's face.

'The fun way,' he heard himself say.

Gwen led him to a far back corner of the cave.

She stopped in front of a circular hole in the rock floor about as wide as his bedroom mat. They waited. After about thirty seconds there was a loud shuddering 'whoompf' from deep below them and a spray of water flew up out of the hole and splattered on the roof of the cave. Then there was an even louder sucking noise and the water disappeared.

'Right,' said Gwen, holding his hand tight. 'Next time it does that, after the water stops spraying, we jump in.'

Jump in?

Jake spent the next thirty seconds trying to think up an excuse to go back to the safe way. The best he could come up with was 'I feel sick', but before he could get it out the 'whoompf' happened again, the water stopped spraying, and Gwen jumped, taking him with her.

Jake's hand slipped from hers, and for a few panicked seconds he felt himself being sucked downwards into watery darkness by an incredible force. Then his hand was in hers again and the ride of his life started.

'Arghhhhhhh,' he screamed, mouth closed, eyes wide with amazement. He wasn't going down any more, the tunnel had curved and he was hurtling along sideways, dazzled by the colours blurring past him in the whooshing water.

This is it, he thought. This is what those giant water rides on those world's biggest amusement parks on satellite TV must be like.

Only this is better.

Then it was over. Suddenly Jake felt himself spinning in dark, deep, churning water.

The excitement faded.

Panic took its place.

He was out of air. He could see daylight, far far above. The agony in his chest was making him curl up.

'I won't make it,' he thought. 'Got to breathe. Got to . . .'

He breathed in.

Not water, air.

Air?

His eyes shifted focus and he saw why. Gwen's eyes were millimetres from his. She was right in front of him, her hands under his arms, her face pressed to his, her mouth over his mouth and nose.

He was breathing her air.

It smelt faintly of bubblegum.

Jake had seen a lot of kissing on satellite TV, and most of it hadn't made him feel that good. If he had seen a girl put her mouth over a boy's mouth and nose, he would probably have thrown up.

But now he didn't care.

Gwen was kicking them both towards the surface and he felt good.

Having a real live friend was everything he'd ever dreamed of.

More.

Suddenly Jake knew everything was going to be OK.

With Gwen's help, he thought happily, I'll get Crusher back for sure. Once the magazine people have written their glowing article about the business, and it's printed and they can't change it, we'll go to the city and break into their place and bring Crusher back.

And in the meantime he'd help Mabel find Alfonse, even if he had to turn the island upside down.

And, thought Jake, as he and Gwen burst through the water into sunlight, even if it turns out Mum and Dad had happy childhoods and they just didn't want me, even that won't be quite so bad with Gwen around.

Gwen pulled her mouth away and felt around with her tongue for the bubblegum and started chewing again.

She wiped his face.

'Sorry about the dribble,' she said.

Suddenly, unexpectedly, Jake felt embarrassed. He looked at his feet as he and Gwen sloshed their way onto dry land and flopped down onto a sun-warm rock without speaking.

This is stupid, thought Jake. She saved my life. What's embarrassing about that?

He looked at her face, pale in the sunlight, and he felt warm all over and it wasn't just the sun. It was because she was the first real live friend he'd ever had and he couldn't imagine having a better one.

'Thanks,' he said.

'No problem,' she said with a grin. Then she looked serious again. 'I think I know someone who can prove to you that your parents did want you.'

Jake stared at her. How did she know about that? He hadn't said anything about it, only thought it.

Is that what real live friends could do? Know each other's thoughts?

He was about to ask her when another thought hit him. An even more urgent one.

'How did you stay underwater that long?' he asked. 'How did you share your air with me for all those minutes and not die?'

Gwen dropped her eyes and studied her wet pink dress for a long time. She picked at a scab on her knee. Jake was worried she'd make it bleed, but she stopped in time.

He could see she was thinking hard about her answer.

Finally she shrugged and looked at him with a sad smile.

'Simple,' she said. 'I'm already dead.'

FIFTEEN

Jake stared at her.

For a crazy second he'd thought she'd said 'dead'.

He tilted his head to let the seawater run out of his ears, and wondered what word Gwen could have said that sounded like 'dead'.

Then he realised she was still speaking.

'I died forty-two years ago,' she said. 'Mabel died forty-three years ago.'

Jake prodded frantically in his ears to find the seaweed that was blocking his hearing and making him think Gwen was saying crazy things.

His ears were empty.

No seaweed.

Oh no, thought Jake in sudden panic, I must have suffered oxygen deprivation from being underwater too long and I've got brain damage.

Gwen reached over and put her hand on his arm.

His panic went.

'Jake,' she said, 'it's OK. You haven't got brain damage.'

She took her hand away.

The panic came back.

She must have it, he thought miserably. She gave me too much of her air and she's got brain damage.

Jake realised she was still speaking. The least he could do, after everything she'd done for him, was humour the poor thing. She may be having delusions, but she was still his friend.

'When our mother died,' Gwen was saying, 'our father put us in a home in the city. Me and Mabel.'

'Right,' said Jake.

'I was six and Mabel was three,' said Gwen. 'It wasn't a bad place. The people running it were pretty kind. Then we got moved to this one.'

She pointed up the cliff in the direction of the house.

'Right,' said Jake.

He heard his voice wobble a bit. It was her eyes. There was so much sadness in them.

'The people here,' she said, 'weren't kind.'

Jake saw anger flash across her face.

'They were religious,' she said, 'but they didn't like children very much.'

'Right,' said Jake, head spinning. Where had he heard that before?

'Mabel died when she was seven,' said Gwen.

'After that I tried to escape, but they caught me and brought me back. I got sick, so they had to shift me to the mainland, to a hospital. I didn't get better. I died when I was eleven.'

Jake tried to say 'right' but he couldn't. His throat had sort of closed over.

This is incredible, he thought. I'm sitting here getting upset at a story. She should write books.

'At first,' said Gwen, 'I didn't like being dead. Then I found Mabel and it got better. Now we spend our time with all the other unwanted kids. Sometimes it's good fun.'

Jake didn't say 'right' because it wasn't, it was tragic. She obviously believed everything she was saying.

'Mabel always wanted to come back here,' she continued, 'to find her friend Alfonse, but we didn't know the way. Then a few weeks ago we felt the sadness.'

Jake looked at her, confused.

'When you've been very sad yourself,' said Gwen, 'you can spot other people's sadness a long way off. It guided us here.'

Jake tried to understand what she meant.

Could she mean me, he thought. Could she mean they're here because of my sadness?

For a few seconds the thought made him want to cry.

Then he remembered it couldn't possibly have happened.

'I know you think I'm a mental case,' said Gwen. 'Would it help if we talk to someone you know, someone who was in the home here with me and Mabel?'

'Who?' said Jake.

'Bernie,' said Gwen.

Jake looked at her, puzzled.

'Bernie Goff,' said Gwen.

As they made their way along the path to the jetty, Jake was deep in thought. He hoped Gwen's parents could afford the best mental treatment for their daughter. Perhaps, if Mum and Dad offered the medical team a free holiday, they'd do it cut-price.

Suddenly Gwen pushed Jake behind some bushes and dragged him down onto the dirt. He pulled himself free and looked at her in alarm. Brain damage could lead to sudden violence, he'd seen it on TV.

It was tragic. She was the best person he'd ever met in his whole life and he didn't want to have to fight her.

'This isn't a fight,' hissed Gwen. She pointed to the brow of the next hill.

Jake peered through the leaves.

The magazine people were setting off on a walk. The magazine man, wearing Dad's hiking shoes, was peering around and writing in a note-book. The magazine woman was wearing Mum's elastic-sided boots and carrying Crusher.

Jake stared miserably at the little furry figure with his head jammed under the magazine woman's arm. He hoped she was wearing deodorant.

Hang on, Crusher, he said silently. I'll get you back, I promise. Once all this is over.

Jake whistled a TV jingle to help Crusher hang on. Gwen was looking at him, but he didn't care. He just hoped his whistling and his love were strong enough to penetrate the magazine woman's armpit.

The magazine people disappeared over the brow of the hill and Gwen stood up.

Suddenly Jake remembered he'd never told Gwen why she and Mabel must stay out of sight of the adults.

Better tell her now.

He wondered if her fragile mental state would allow her to take it all in.

He had to try.

Then he saw she was looking at him.

'It's OK,' she said. 'I know.'

Mr Goff clung onto a jetty post as if his legs had turned into jellyfish. Then he sat down on the old bed he'd been carrying to his boat and stared at Gwen, his mouth moving but not making any sound.

Jake watched anxiously, wondering if there was any medication he should be helping Mr Goff take.

Finally Mr Goff spoke.

'Gwen,' he croaked. 'Gwen Neary.'

'Hello Bernie,' said Gwen. 'Sorry if I scared you.'

'You . . . you got sick and they sent you back to the mainland,' said Mr Goff, screwing up his face as if he was struggling with the memory. He looked at Gwen for a long time and tears started to roll down his bristly cheeks. 'You didn't get better,' he said softly.

Gwen smiled sadly at him.

'It's OK,' she said. 'I'm with Mabel.'

Mr Goff's face lit up. 'Mabel,' he said. Then his face fell again. 'Poor little beggar.'

Jake realised he was holding onto a jetty post too. His legs were pretty wobbly as well. He tried to remember if he'd ever seen anything on TV about group delusions. Two or more people imagining exactly the same thing at the same time.

He couldn't.

'Bernie,' said Gwen. 'You were around here when Jake was born. Did his parents want him?'

Jake stared at her. What was she doing?

Mr Goff looked out to sea for quite a while. Then he turned back to them.

'I wish I could say yes,' he said, not looking at Jake. 'But I don't honestly know. They kept to themselves mostly. I know when they first came here they weren't planning on having kids. And the way they've treated the poor bloke since . . .'

He spat into the water.

Jake suddenly felt he wanted to leave. He took a step, but Gwen put her hand on his arm and suddenly he didn't feel so bad.

'I'm glad you got off the island alive, Bernie,' said Gwen.

Mr Goff smiled sadly.

'I'm alive,' he said, 'but I haven't really got off the island, have I? I'm here four times a week.'

Gwen smiled back at him. 'Don't worry,' she said. 'Some things take time.'

Mr Goff turned to Jake.

'She was always like that,' he said. 'Cheering us up when things were tough. If she's your friend now, you're a lucky bloke. Don't fight it. You've had a rough trot and you deserve her.'

He ruffled Jake's hair.

Jake nodded as if he understood.

He wished he did.

But he didn't.

Poor Gwen was suffering from oxygen deprivation, that's why she was having these delusions, but what was Mr Goff's excuse?

As Jake and Gwen walked up to the house, Jake realised what he wanted most in the world, apart from Crusher and parents who loved him. It was to go and have a lie down, and when he got up, for everything to be back to normal. For Gwen's brain to have got better. For Gwen and Mabel's parents to have turned up. For Mum and Dad to invite the whole family for a long holiday after the magazine people had gone. For he and Gwen to have heaps of time to get to know each other properly.

'A lie down would be good for you too,' he said to Gwen. 'Somewhere quiet, like your parents' boat. Or you could use the Pink Room, that's quiet.'

'Thanks,' said Gwen, 'but I've got to find Mabel.'

Jake's insides lurched as he followed her into the house. He'd forgotten about Mabel. She could be pestering Mum and Dad about Alfonse at this very moment.

Luckily she wasn't.

Mum and Dad were busy in the office.

'I think she's up here,' whispered Gwen, pointing up the stairs.

They crept up.

Gwen stopped outside the Blue Room.

'This used to be the punishment room in the home,' she said. 'We were put in here for days sometimes. One time, to give myself something to do, I scratched a message on the wall for the other kids to see. "We'll all be free one day," I wrote. The people running the place saw it and scrubbed it out and kept me in here for an extra week.'

Jake saw Gwen's eyes flash.

'So I got my hand through the window bars,' she continued, 'and scratched it again on the outside wall.'

Jake stared at her. That must have been what Mum was doing up the ladder. Scrubbing it off so the magazine people wouldn't see it.

Except she couldn't have, because none of this was true.

Suddenly from inside the Blue Room came a faint and tearful voice.

'I want Alfonse.'

'Mabel,' said Gwen, and went in.

Jake followed her.

Whoever Alfonse is, he thought, I wish he'd turn up. With a bit of luck he might know where Gwen's parents are and whether they've got private medical insurance.

Inside the room, Jake looked around, puzzled. He couldn't see Mabel anywhere. Not in the ensuite, not under the bed, not behind the dresser. The wardrobe door was open and she wasn't in there.

Then he saw Gwen looking upwards.

He looked up too.

And gasped.

High over the bed, her little face streaked with tears, was Mabel.

For a second, Jake thought she was hooked on the ceiling somehow. But she wasn't. He could see daylight between her and the plaster. No hook. No rope. No superglue.

She was floating in the air.

Her tears were forming drips on her chin and dropping onto the bed. Jake could see the big damp patch they were making on the sheet.

He didn't look at the damp patch for long. His eyes shot back up to the incredible sight on the ceiling, his brain struggling to make sense of it.

'I thought she'd be here,' said Gwen. 'She's been here a bit lately. It was where she died.'

As this sank in, Jake looked up at the silent anguish on Mabel's face.

Then he looked at Gwen as she climbed onto a bedside cabinet and reached up to her little sister.

His own silent anguish started.

There was no other explanation.

He had to accept it.

His first ever real live friend was a ghost.

SIXTEEN

Jake ran.

He ran out of the house into the side garden, squeezed through the hedge into the ti-tree grove, flung himself between the trunks and branches, and slithered down through the tangled undergrowth to the side beach.

He didn't care how scraped or ripped he got.

What did it matter?

All he'd wanted was a friend and instead he'd got a nightmare.

He threw himself down on the sand and pressed his face into a pile of seaweed. It was slimy and smelly but at least it was real live seaweed, not seaweed that had died forty-two years ago.

OK, it was very smelly. And Jake could tell it didn't give two sucks of a sea slug that he was feeling bad.

It might be real and live, thought Jake miserably, but I bet it doesn't give people presents to cheer them up. Or share oxygen with them when they desperately need it.

Jake flopped over and lay with his cheek on the wet sand, staring out to sea.

He tried to think of happy things like rolling down sand dunes and staring at ants with Crusher, but things Gwen had said kept barging into his mind.

Something about being with all the other unwanted kids.

Something about it being fun.

What unwanted kids?

Where?

Jake's thoughts started to ebb and flow with the waves that were hissing towards him across the sand.

He tried to imagine what it would be like to be surrounded by other kids.

Other unwanted kids, just like him.

Kids like Gwen.

Never lonely again.

Forever.

That, thought Jake as his eyelids started to get heavy and the waves started to sound like voices whispering his name, that would really be living.

Even if you were dead.

'Jake, wake up.'

Jake opened his eyes.

He blinked a few times.

Gwen was looking down at him. Behind her was the blue sky. He could hear kids' voices, laughing and chattering.

Jake sat up.

He was cold from the wet sand and his back was stiff.

But when he looked around he forgot all about that.

He stared, gobsmacked.

There were kids all over his beach. Kids of all ages, running around having fun in tatty old fashioned clothes. Playing with his boogie board and fishing gear and beach tennis and snorkle set.

A boy nearby was building a medieval sandcastle, using Jake's bait spade to carefully carve out the battlements. Jake's plastic Star Wars action figures were already in position in the castle. The boy glanced up and saw Jake.

'Hey,' yelled the boy to the other kids. 'He's awake.'

Before Jake knew what was happening, he was surrounded by kids, staring at him, grinning, whispering to each other.

Jake looked around for Gwen, but he couldn't see her.

'Thanks for letting us use your stuff,' said the sandcastle boy. 'We haven't got stuff like this where we are.'

'Yeah,' said a girl with a hair curl over one eye

and a bruise over the other. 'We haven't got parents who spoil us.'

'Ignore her,' said a boy with a friendly face and half of one ear missing. 'We'd give anything to have parents like yours.'

The other kids murmured their agreement.

Jake was about to put them straight about Mum and Dad, but he found that the muscles in his throat had seized up with shock.

'It's still pretty good, but, where we are,' said a girl with frizzy ginger hair and painful-looking red marks on her hands. 'Specially since the Internet.'

The other kids all laughed.

'Yeah,' said the sandcastle boy. Jake saw he had the same bruises on his legs as Gwen. 'It's good fun these days. All the e-mails come through us. We make sure they all go to the, um, right addresses.'

More laughter.

What does he mean? thought Jake. Then he remembered the e-mail that had gone to the travel magazine.

'Viruses,' said a girl with several teeth missing. 'We have heaps of fun with them.'

'Websites that eat credit cards,' said an angry-looking boy with a bandaged chest. He grinned. 'I invented those.'

'OK everyone,' said a voice loudly. 'Back off and let him breathe.'

Jake realised he hadn't taken a breath for a while. He took one, and saw with relief that the voice was Gwen's.

She knelt in front of him on the sand.

'Jake,' she said, 'this is Polly.' She pulled an earnest-looking girl in a grubby blue cardigan closer to Jake. 'Polly was in the home with me and Mabel. She found her way back to the island around the time you were born.'

'I came back to look for a key,' said Polly. She held out her arm. Jake saw that round her wrist was a length of rusty chain held in place by a padlock. 'I didn't find one,' she added.

Jake reached out slowly and touched the padlock. It was rusted over.

Gwen put her arm round Polly.

'Tell Jake how his parents felt when he was born,' said Gwen.

Polly nodded vigorously, face glowing with memories.

'They were so pleased,' she said. 'Your mum and dad. Over the moon. Tickled pink. They wanted you so much. We were really jealous.'

The other kids all murmured agreement.

Jake stared at them, struggling to take it in.

They were all ghosts.

He was surrounded by ghosts.

Polly was still gazing at him, her pale face shining. She looked like an ordinary kid thinking about something she really wanted.

Suddenly Jake didn't care if Polly was a ghost or Gwen was a ghost.

He just wanted to believe them.

'Thankyou,' he said to them both, his eyes hot and his voice thick.

Before he could suggest taking Polly to Mr Goff so Mr Goff could remove the padlock with WD40 and a hacksaw, Gwen spoke again.

'Jake,' she said gently. 'There's one more thing you should know. It's about Alfonse.'

Jake saw that Mabel, face still tear-streaked, was standing at Gwen's shoulder.

'The reason Mabel came back for Alfonse,' said Gwen, 'is that he helped her when she was very sad and lonely. Specially when she was locked up on her own. Teddy bears can be really good at that, eh?'

Jake felt cold dread seep through him. He saw the way Gwen was looking at him, and suddenly he had a strong feeling he didn't want to hear any more.

'Just before Mabel died,' continued Gwen, 'they took Alfonse away from her and shut him away. That was when she promised him she'd come back for him.'

Gwen looked at Jake for what felt to him, as his panic rose, like ages.

'You can understand that, can't you,' she said gently.

'Alfonse has got a scar on his face,' said the girl with frizzy hair. 'I sewed it up for Mabel.'

Jake stood up.

'I've got to go,' he shouted.

Frantically he pushed his way through the kids and started running across the sand.

It was crazy. What would a bunch of ghosts know anyway. Making up stories about important stuff just for a laugh. First rule of hotel management. Never trust anybody involved with computer viruses. Specially not anything they say about parents or teddy bears.

He reached the undergrowth at the base of the slope that led up to the house and started clawing his way up through it.

I'll find out the truth, thought Jake grimly. I'll find it out from Mum and Dad.

SEVENTEEN

Mum and Dad were still in the office.

As Jake burst in, he saw them sitting together, heads bent over what he assumed was the bookings book.

Then he saw it was the photo album, open at his baby photos.

Mum had tears in her eyes.

She and Dad looked up, startled.

'Why didn't you tell me,' said Jake. 'Why didn't you tell me Crusher belongs to someone else?'

They stared at him, even more startled.

'What do you mean,' said Dad.

Mum put her hand on Dad's arm. 'Let me, Frank,' she said. 'Jake, love, I didn't want to give Crusher to Kevin and Fiona. I did it for all of us.'

'I don't mean that,' said Jake. 'I mean why didn't you tell me Crusher's real name is Alfonse. Why didn't you tell me he belongs to a kid from the children's home.'

Mum and Dad looked at each other.

'But he doesn't,' said Dad. 'Does he?'

'How did you find out?' said Mum to Jake. 'How did you find out about the children's home?'

Jake looked at them sadly. They still couldn't get their story straight.

'I know everything,' said Jake. 'The furniture in the bottom cellar, Mr Goff being Bernie, the ghost kids . . .'

Mum was so startled by this she dropped the photo album. 'Ghost kids,' she said, standing up. 'What ghost kids?'

Suddenly Jake couldn't stand it any more. He just wanted to get to the truth. Even if it changed their lives forever.

'I'll show you,' he said.

Dad leaped to his feet, alarmed, and dropped what he'd been holding.

Jake saw it was Gwen's cardboard doll.

What ghost kids, thought Jake scornfully. You know perfectly well what ghost kids. OK, let's see you pretend you don't know when they're right in front of you.

He turned and headed out the door.

'Jake,' said Mum. 'Where are you going?'

He didn't reply. He just glanced over his shoulder to make sure they were following, then headed for the side garden.

*　　*　　*

Jake waited for Mum and Dad to struggle through the hole in the hedge. When they'd made it into the ti-trees, he picked his way between the trunks and branches to a place where they'd all be able to look down onto the beach.

Just before he got there, Dad gave a yell.

Jake looked back. Dad was holding his head where he'd banged it on a branch. Jake took a step towards him, concerned.

Then stopped. It's not bleeding, he thought, and there are more important things to worry about. That was the trouble with parents, you cared about them even when they'd been lying to you.

Mum and Dad struggled over to him.

'Jake,' said Mum, 'What are you doing? Come back inside. You mustn't be seen. We mustn't be seen with you.'

Jake tried to keep his voice calm.

'You reckon you don't know what ghost kids I'm talking about,' he said. 'So I've brought you here to show you. Now perhaps you'll tell me the truth. About Crusher.' He took a deep breath. 'And about me.'

He turned and pointed down at the beach.

And felt his mouth drop open helplessly.

The beach was deserted.

The ghost kids had vanished.

Jake took a step closer to the top of the slope, straining to see if the ghost kids were hiding behind the rocks.

They weren't.

The beach was completely empty.

Or was it?

Jake pushed a branch away from in front of his eyes and suddenly saw, sitting on the sand, three figures.

With a cold sick feeling rising in his guts, Jake recognized them.

One was Crusher.

The other two were the magazine people. They were building a sandcastle. With the bait spade and bucket. Strewn around them on the sand were the boogie board and fishing gear and beach tennis stuff and snorkle set.

And, thought Jake, weak with despair, my Star Wars figures.

It was all over.

The magazine people must know there was a kid on the island.

They knew the exclusive adults-only retreat was a fake and a sham. And that's what they'd be writing in their article.

Unless, thought Jake, I can stop them.

He flung himself down the slope, crashing through the undergrowth. He was getting even more scraped and ripped than last time, but he didn't care.

I'll explain to them, he thought wildly as fronds lashed his legs and branches whacked him in the face. I'll explain everything and they'll understand.

They've got to. They were kids once. They're building a sandcastle. They can't be all bad.

He burst out of the undergrowth and sprinted across the sand towards the magazine people.

Crusher saw him first and even though Crusher didn't show it, Jake felt the relief and love radiating from Crusher's furry, stitched-up face.

Then the magazine people saw him.

'Hello,' said the magazine man, holding the plastic spade frozen in mid-pat. 'What have we got here?'

The magazine woman dropped the bucket and gawped. 'I told you,' she said to the magazine man. 'I told you.'

Jake took a deep breath.

'I'm not going to try and lie to you,' he said, looking them in the face. 'I'm a kid.'

He waited a moment for this to fully sink in, then continued.

'It's not Mum and Dad's fault,' he said. 'They didn't want me. I was an accident. If you don't believe me, look in their photo album. They'd had such an unhappy childhood they decided never to have kids of their own. They were devastated when I came along. It totally ruined all their plans for an exclusive adults-only holiday facility. Don't punish them more by writing a bad article, please. They've suffered enough having me.'

Jake stopped, too out of breath and too miserable to continue.

The magazine people were staring at him, open-mouthed.

I think it's working, thought Jake. First rule of hotel management. Always tell the truth.

Then he heard a moan from behind him.

He spun round. It was Mum, eyes wide and tearful. She and Dad must have followed him down.

'Jake,' she said, coming towards him. 'It's not true. We did want you, love. We did.'

Don't, thought Jake desperately. Don't spoil it. I've told the truth and it's working. Don't spoil it with lies.

Mum turned to the magazine people. 'We wanted a baby so much,' she said. 'We tried to have one for years. But the doctors said it was impossible for us. That's why we came here and started an adults-only guesthouse. To get away from children. Seeing other children was too painful for us because we so desperately wanted one of our own.'

Mum, pleaded Jake silently. Don't. No more stories. Next she'd be telling them she had a really happy childhood.

'We thought it was hopeless,' said Dad.

'We thought we'd never have what our parents had,' continued Mum. 'A much-loved son or daughter.' Her face lit up through her tears. 'And then, about a year after we arrived, miraculously, I got pregnant.'

'The doctors said it was an accident,' said Dad. 'I mean, it happened in the normal way, but after all the trouble we'd had, they said it was an accident of nature.'

Jake stared at him.

'That's why we called you our little accident,' said Mum.

There was a silence. Nobody spoke. Only the waves made a sound, and they seemed to be sighing like people do when they hear something they've never thought of before.

Keep going, said Jake silently, chest thumping. I want to hear more.

The magazine people looked as though they did too.

'We shouldn't have carried on with the guesthouse,' said Mum. 'But we didn't have a choice.'

'We'd borrowed so much money from the bank,' said Dad, 'we were scared to walk away. Even though we knew this wasn't a good place for a kid.'

Jake couldn't stay silent any longer.

'If you wanted me,' he said, 'why were you so miserable? I saw the photos.'

Mum stroked Jake's cheek. 'I was being greedy,' she said. 'Having you around was such a joy, I wanted more. I wanted another baby. And I wanted a brother or sister for you so you wouldn't be so lonely here.' Mum looked down at something in her hand. Jake saw it was Gwen's cardboard doll.

'But,' said Mum, 'it didn't happen.'

Jake suddenly felt like he needed a slow-motion replay of the last few minutes, just to take everything in. He felt weak and shaky all over, like he'd been chained to a bed for most of his life.

Mum turned to the magazine people. 'There's lots we've done that we shouldn't have,' she said. 'But the thing we most shouldn't have done was give you Crusher.'

She stepped over and picked Crusher up and brushed the sand off his head.

'Crusher's the one who's helped Jake get though the last eleven years,' she said, 'and we should never have taken him away from Jake.'

Jake held his breath.

'Kevin and Fiona,' said Mum, 'write what you like, but we're taking Crusher back.'

'That's right,' said Dad. 'Write what you like, we don't care. But it would be good if you could mention the cooking.'

Jake didn't hear much of what was said next because after Mum handed Crusher to him he spent the next few minutes with his face buried in Crusher's fur.

'Sorry Crusher', he whispered. 'After all this time apart, the first thing I do is make you soggy.'

He could tell Crusher understood.

Then Jake looked up and saw the magazine

people walking away towards the house. He saw something else. The sandcastle they'd been building was in the shape of the island. It was a pretty good likeness, except for one thing. They'd got the house wrong. Instead of one building they'd got about four.

Jake didn't have a chance to look at it for long because Mum and Dad both put their arms round him and Crusher.

'We're sorry,' said Mum.

'Incredibly sorry,' said Dad. 'Incredibly. Incredibly. Incredibly.'

Jake realised, as the four of them stood there on the sand hugging, that it felt more like a family than he could ever remember. Specially as all four of them were sobbing.

And a little while later, when Jake opened his eyes and blinked the tears away and peered over Mum's shoulder and saw two faces watching them from the undergrowth, he felt as if Gwen and Mabel were part of the family too.

EIGHTEEN

Jake walked with Crusher up and down the beach for a long time, trying to find a solution.

He couldn't.

Every argument he came up with fell flat.

Nothing he could think of would make the awful truth go away. Sometimes the truth could make you feel really sick.

'I've got a mum and dad,' Jake said to Crusher at last. 'She hasn't. She needs you more than I do.'

Even through his tears he could tell Crusher understood.

So he didn't bother trying to come up with any more arguments. He spent the rest of the time swapping memories with Crusher of all the things they'd done together.

The adventures they'd shared.

The joy and sadness they'd been through.

The ants they'd stared at.

The bank robberies they hadn't actually done

but had enjoyed thinking about.

Then it was time to say goodbye.

'Thankyou Crusher,' whispered Jake. 'I'll always love you.'

He could tell Crusher felt the same.

Jake gave Crusher one last hug, then walked over to where Gwen and Mabel were waiting at the edge of the beach. As he got closer, he saw Mabel's dark eyes fixed on Crusher. They were slowly widening, as if she couldn't believe what was happening.

Jake held Crusher out to her.

'Alfonse,' she whispered.

She reached out and took Crusher and hugged him tight. For the first time since Jake had met her, a smile crept across her face and her eyes shone with happiness.

Then she did something that Jake knew, even as he stared in stunned amazement, he would remember for as long as he lived, and possibly longer.

She held Crusher in front of her face and whistled softly to him.

It wasn't a TV jingle but it was just as good.

Even though sadness was gripping his throat, Jake could tell that Crusher was enjoying the moment too. Despite the inconvenience of having to get used to his old name.

Jake felt Gwen step close to him and gently touch his arm.

'Thankyou Jake,' she said softly. 'Mabel will always be grateful to you. I will too.'

She wasn't grinning at him like she usually did. She was smiling a soft smile that made Jake want to have her around forever.

'Some of the kids didn't think you'd give him back,' she said. 'But I knew you would. I knew you'd turn out to be that sort of person.'

Jake didn't quite understand what she meant, but there was something more important he had to ask her.

'Will we see each other again?'

'I hope so,' she said. 'One day.'

She pressed something into Jake's hand. Before he had a chance to look down to see what it was, he heard someone sob behind him.

He turned and was surprised to see Mum and Dad standing a short distance away on the sand, watching. He was sure they'd gone back up to the house after the magazine couple.

Mum was clutching Dad's arm, staring at Gwen and Mabel in tearful amazement.

'Frank,' she said. 'Look. It's happening again.'

Jake didn't understand what Mum was rabbiting on about. Right now, though, he had more things to ask Gwen.

He turned back.

Gwen was gone.

So were Mabel and Crusher.

Jake struggled not to call out Crusher's name.

He looked down to see what Gwen had put in his hand.

It was a piece of bubblegum, still wet and warm.

Jake plonked the last of the magazine people's bags down on the jetty.

At least now he was an official member of the family he could help Dad with the bags.

That was one consolation.

Not much of a one, thought Jake, given that the magazine people are probably going to write an article that'll make us bankrupt.

Mr Goff came up from below decks and Mum and Dad said g'day to him, but Jake could tell their hearts weren't really in it.

Jake tried to be optimistic. Perhaps, he thought, the magazine people had a really good time playing with my stuff on the beach. Perhaps they've remembered how much fun they had as kids. Perhaps they'll write really nice things about how good this place is for relieving executive stress.

The magazine people came striding down from the house. They didn't look like people who'd rediscovered the joys of childhood.

'Bye, Kevin and Fiona,' said Dad. 'We do hope you enjoyed your stay.'

Jake felt proud at what a brave face Dad was putting on.

The magazine man looked at Mum and Dad for a long moment. 'Frank,' he said, 'Maureen, I'm not going to beat around the bush. As an exclusive adults-only holiday retreat, this place sucks.'

Jake saw Mum and Dad both slump visibly, as if someone had whacked them across the back with a big leather strap.

'Bluntly,' continued the magazine man, 'our readers expect something a little more from a sophisticated adult establishment than rolling down sand dunes, treading in what appears to be rotting Easter eggs, and prodding seaweed with sticks.'

'Oysters,' said Jake before he could stop himself. What hope do we have, he thought gloomily, if they can't even get that right.

'And Frank,' said the magazine woman, 'our sophisticated international readers expect something a bit better in their pancakes than seaweed.'

'And,' said the magazine man, looking at Jake, 'finding the place crawling with kids.'

'And nearly drowning in a cave,' said the magazine woman.

The magazine man glared at her. She blushed deep red.

'OK,' said Mum. 'That's enough. You didn't like it here and you're going to write bad things about us and we'll never get another booking again. We get the message. Rather than standing around here insulting my family, I think you'd better leave.'

'Engines all fired up and raring to go,' muttered Mr Goff. 'It could be a bumpy trip.'

I don't get it, thought Jake. They really liked the place when they first arrived. When I was under the bed they were raving about it.

What was going on?

Then Jake remembered the movie he'd seen on TV about the explorers. When they'd discovered an ancient tribe's gold mine, they'd threatened to blow it up if the tribe didn't sell it to them.

Jake held his breath.

'Of course,' said the magazine man, 'there is another way this could turn out.'

Jake could see Mum and Dad still didn't know what was going on.

'You could sell us the lease to this place,' said the magazine man.

'OK,' said Jake.

'What?' said Dad.

Mum, stunned but starting to look delighted, put her hand over Jake's mouth.

'We know some investors who want to get into up-market accommodation,' said the magazine man. 'With the right people behind it, this place could be a quality boutique executive resort.'

'And who says we're not the right people,' growled Dad.

'We do,' said Mum, looking as though she was about to push Dad into the water.

'She's right,' said the magazine man. 'You

haven't got a clue. You think small. You need at least twenty rooms to make this place pay. Plus you've got a kid. And you don't even charge for drinks.'

Even though Jake didn't like hearing Dad's faults being discussed like this, he felt his heart trying to do a happy dance with his kidneys.

'What sort of money are we talking about?' said Dad.

'Enough to pay off the bank,' said the magazine man.

Jake caught Mum's eye and he could see she felt the same as he did. Like doing a jig down the jetty and a quick bit of jazz ballet with Mr Goff.

'We'd want more than that,' said Dad.

Jake flinched. That's it, he thought. He's headed for the water. With a lobster pot jammed on his privates.

Before Mum could do anything, though, the magazine man looked hard at Dad.

'How much more?' he said.

'Enough for a deposit on a small motel on the mainland,' said Dad.

The magazine man thought for a moment. 'OK,' he said. 'I think we can say yes to that.'

It was only later, after the magazine people had gone and Dad had cooked lobster and chips for dinner and Mum had made mango cream tarts and they'd all made lots of excited plans about moving to the mainland, that Jake had a thought that made him smile a lot.

All those up-market child-free executives. He hoped they had fun meeting the ghost kids.

Then Jake stopped smiling because suddenly he'd had an awful thought.

He sat staring at his plate, mango cream curdling in his guts.

What if leaving the island meant he never saw Gwen and Mabel and Crusher again?

NINETEEN

Mr Goff threw another bed onto the fire and the flames roared high into the night sky.

Jake threw the last of the desks on and the flames shot even higher.

I don't get it, thought Jake. I was sure Gwen and Mabel would come back for this. Burning all the children's home furniture they hated so much.

Mr Goff was having a great time, dancing about, splintering wood with his feet. Even Mum and Dad were enjoying themselves. These days they were more romantic together than Jake had ever seen them.

Jake sighed.

Two weeks since he'd given Crusher to Mabel, and not a sign of them.

He'd tried everything. E-mails. The school radio. Leaving notes in the Blue Room. Telepathy. He'd even written a message in the sand in huge letters.

Gwen, where are you?

Nothing.

Not even a sprinkle of icing sugar on the stair carpet.

The weird thing was, even though he was missing Crusher heaps, he was missing Gwen more.

Jake put his hand in his pocket and felt the lump of bubblegum. It was cold and hard now. Not much to remember your first ever real live friend by.

He peered across the dark water at the distant star-swept horizon.

No sign of them.

'I just don't get it,' said Jake.

He had persuaded Dad to have the bonfire on the highest point of the island, even though it had taken them hours to carry all the furniture up here. Flames this size would be visible from hundreds of kilometres away.

Thousands probably.

So why weren't they here?

'What don't you get?' asked Mum, slipping her arm round Jake's shoulders. Dad put his arm round from the other side.

'I know sadness attracts them,' said Jake. 'And I'm feeling pretty sad at the moment. So where are they?'

'Give them time,' said Mum. 'We're not moving for a few months yet. They'll be back.'

She kissed him on the hair. Dad squeezed him hard.

That's probably the trouble, thought Jake as he cuddled into them both. I'm not sad enough.

He stared past the leaping flames up at the stars. He decided to ask Mum about something he'd been puzzling over for the last two weeks.

'Mum,' he said. 'On the beach that day, just after I said goodbye to Crusher, why did you say "it's happening again"?'

Mum didn't answer for quite a while.

From her body movements, Jake guessed Mum was swapping looks with Dad.

'It's a bit hard to put into words, love,' she said at last. 'I'm not sure if I really know why myself. Let's wait and see. Perhaps one day we'll understand.'

TWENTY

Jake stood in the back of the boat as it chugged away from the jetty, staring at the island.

The sun was setting. The house and the hills and the rocky outcrops were silhouetted against a flaming sky.

'Goodbye Crusher,' whispered Jake. 'I hope you're happy with Mabel.'

He closed his eyes and concentrated hard. And deep inside he had the faint but definite feeling that Crusher was happy.

Jake opened his eyes, wiped them dry, and looked again at the pink sky.

'Goodbye Gwen,' he whispered. 'I wish I'd seen you again.'

'Hang on everyone,' yelled Mr Goff with the cheerful tone of a man who'd decided to retire and sail round Australia. 'Full steam ahead.'

Jake hung on.

All around him, furniture and suitcases and

cardboard boxes hung on too.

I knew this bit would be hard, thought Jake. Leaving for the last time. Wondering why Gwen never came back. But I didn't know it would hurt this much.

He was glad now he'd tried to be as busy as possible over the past few weeks. Packing. Burying Easter eggs. Making trips to the mainland with Mum and Dad to enrol in the local school and find a motel.

He'd tried not to think about Gwen, and mostly he hadn't. Except for those times Mum and Dad left him in milk bars for hours while they went off for business meetings or something. Then he'd thought about her a lot. Even double thickshakes hadn't taken away the pain then.

He'd thought about something else too.

What Mum had meant by 'it's happening again'.

What had seeing Gwen and Mabel reminded her of that had happened before?

And why is it, thought Jake now, staring at the dark outline of the receding island, that I get a funny feeling whenever I ask myself that?

Perhaps I did get brain damage under the water.

Or bubblegum poisoning.

His thoughts were interrupted by Mum and Dad coming to the back of the boat. He could see they were feeling good about leaving the island, and he knew they wanted him to as well.

He tried to smile, but his face felt harder to stretch than the cold bubblegum in his pocket.

Mum and Dad weren't having that trouble. Their faces were stretching all over the place. Dad was juggling a grin and a frown. Mum was looking happy, worried and excited all at once.

'Jake,' said Mum. 'We've got some news.'

Jake looked at her and put all his effort into a smile. The new bedspreads for the motel must have arrived.

'I'm going to have a baby,' she said.

Jake stared at her.

'Mum's pregnant,' said Dad.

Jake stared at him.

'Actually,' said Mum, 'I've been pregnant for a while, but we wanted to make sure it was all OK before we told you.'

'And is it?' asked Jake. His voice was trembling.

Mum nodded, eyes shining.

'It's twins,' she said. 'We found out yesterday. Girls.'

'Girls?' said Jake. 'Two girls?'

Mum nodded again.

Jake's heart was suddenly chugging faster than the diesel engine under his feet.

Mum took a deep breath and glanced at Dad. Jake saw Dad squeeze her hand. Mum looked to Jake like she was preparing herself to say something. Something she was a bit nervous about Jake hearing.

'We've decided,' said Mum, 'to call them Gwen and Mabel.'

Jake stood in the spray, his insides churning harder than the water at the back of the boat, and thought about this for a long time.

Mum and Dad were watching him closely, anxiously.

Finally he understood.

'It's happening again?' he said. They both nodded.

Jake took a deep breath.

'Is that what happened with me?'

They both nodded.

For long seconds they were all frozen.

Then Jake decided to leave his past in the past.

He flung his arms round them both and hugged them as hard as he could, tears of joy running hot down his cheeks.

His Mum and Dad.

His new Mum and Dad.

His best Mum and Dad.

And after Mr Goff had yelled that the hot chocolate was ready, and Mum and Dad had gone up front, Jake gazed at the water and thought about his new sisters.

Two girls with dark eyes and the best smiles.

He'd have to keep at least one of them away from bubblegum until she was old enough to chew.

Who knows, Jake thought. I might even see Crusher again.

Then he raised his eyes for one last look at the island.

And saw that the silhouette had changed.

Instead of smooth rounded hills against the pink sky, Jake saw the outlines of figures, tiny in the distance.

Hundreds of children, waving goodbye.

Jake waved back.

He waved until the island had disappeared, and all his old friends too, and the sky had faded.

Then, whistling happily, he went to join Mum and Dad in the front of the boat.